The Santa Rita Payroll

A Western Frontier Adventure

◇

Robert Peecher

For information the author may be contacted at

PO Box 967; Watkinsville GA; 30677

or at mooncalfpress.com

FOR JEAN

PEECHER

- 1 -

Roy Bennett emptied three cans of beans into a pan with a slab of bacon. He speared the bacon with a fork and began cutting slices as the pan heated on the cook stove.

"I'm going out to get the team ready," Clint Thacker said.

Roy had been at this relay station since 1873 when the mine reopened and the Wells, Fargo & Co. stagecoach began running from Santa Rita, down through the mountains, and up to Albuquerque. He'd seen some changes in those eight short years.

For one, Silver City boomed with gold and silver mines all through the mountains to the west. Roy remembered it when it was nothing more than a collection of tents around a single claim. But now it was a full-fledged mountain city.

For another, Albuquerque wasn't Albuquerque no more. Now, Albuquerque was a bustling little stretch of buildings along the terminus of the Atchison, Topeka, and

Santa Fe Railroad, and what used to be Albuquerque was a just an old Spanish mission town around a pretty little plaza not far from the Rio Grande.

Mesilla hadn't changed so much, but El Paso to the south had grown with the railroad, and had a reputation for being more dangerous than even Silver City. Roy had never been to El Paso, and he intended to keep it that way. He was too old to start gunfighting now.

Another change was the railroad creeping toward him. The AT&SF stopped in Albuquerque, but they were laying tracks south of town now. The railroad from Mesilla was almost finished to Deming, and they were saying it wouldn't be long before a narrow-gauge spur was built up to Silver City.

Lots of changes in the last eight years, and there would be more in the next eight. It left a man to worry if his job wasn't going to disappear from under him.

Not that Roy Bennett much got to Mesilla, or Silver City or Albuquerque, or anywhere else, but all his news came from one of those three places.

The Wells Fargo coaches that came through this relay station were bound for Silver City to the west, Albuquerque to the northeast, or Mesilla to the southeast. And when the jehu and shotgun rider stopped for a meal and to change horses, they brought gossip from one of those three places.

Without much else to do, Roy Bennett drank in the gossip. He figured he knew about as much about those three places as any one of the people who lived there.

Sometimes, not usually more than once a year, he'd ride the coach to each of the three towns. He'd seen the depot and the town construction in Albuquerque, but he'd not been there since the trains started running. He'd seen how Mesilla was growing. They were taking water out of the Rio Grande and growing pecans all around Mesilla these days. Most often he went to Silver City when he needed supplies, and he'd usually stay the night and have a drink or two at a saloon there. But a man had to be cautious in Silver City. Half the outlaws in New Mexico Territory got their start in Silver City, Billy Bonney among 'em.

Except for one time when he shot hell out of a rattlesnake, Roy Bennett had never fired his old shotgun in anger, and he didn't intend to if he could help it. He'd never shot at another man, not even an Apache who still today sometimes caused trouble up in the mountains.

Clint Thacker was a younger man, so he usually got the horse teams ready for the stagecoach. Clint was a hard worker. Not but about eighteen years old, he'd been at the relay station for a year now. And a good, hard worker, and Roy Bennett appreciated working with a hard worker more than he appreciated a good meal or a soft bed or a willing woman. Hard workers who toted their weight were a value when hard work had to be done, and running a relay station for Wells, Fargo & Company was no easy job.

Roy had always pitched in and done his best, and he did not see why everyone else shouldn't be expected to do the same.

He sliced the slab of bacon as it started frying in the pan. Bacon grease added flavor to the beans, and the beans would stick with you. Roy knew that some of the relay stations, especially those in cities, offered better meals to travelers, but he wasn't ashamed of a plate of beans and bacon.

From outside the open door, Roy could hear Clint going about his work. Ordering the leaders and the swings and the wheelers. Getting on the collars, hooking up the single trees to the double trees. A man had to know his horses.

Clint talked to the horses while he worked, and Roy appreciated that, too. A good man talked to the horses, got them ready for their work ahead. A man who would talk to a horse – make jokes with them, get them excited about running their route – he was a man who would take decent care of the horses.

The bacon sizzled, and Roy didn't think much of it when he heard a crash from outside. Sometimes people dropped things, and Clint Thacker was not immune to dropping things. Roy went on about his business without giving it another thought.

But after some time – a minute, maybe two – Roy realized that something felt wrong. It took a moment, but he realized that he could no longer hear Clint talking to the horses.

"Clint!" Roy shouted. "Everything all right out there?"

He pushed some beans around to get a slice of bacon into the pan. He enjoyed the way the bacon smelled cooking. Bacon was one of the few things that could kill the smell of the horses in the barn and the smells coming up from the corral. Usually the wind blew the odors down the hill and into the valley, away from the relay station house, but today it was wafting up pretty good.

"Clint?" Roy shouted again, this time turning to look through the wide-open door of the relay station.

Still no answer.

Roy Bennett mixed up the beans and bacon and left them on the stove. Sometimes his knee locked up when he tried to walk, and he found himself now limping as he made his way to the door, trying to stretch out the knee enough to bend it.

Just as he reached the door, a fearsome man with a bandanna tied around his head and shoulder length hair stepped into the doorway. The man had been standing on the other side of the door, waiting in ambush. He was dressed like every Apache warrior Roy Bennett had ever seen or imagined – skin britches, loose shirt, vest, moccasin boots. Roy just got a flash of the man, a speedy image of face shrieking, hatchet raised high, then coming down.

The hatchet struck Roy Bennett in the face, crushing his skull and killing him with one blow.

A couple of men in the barn now appeared with the buckboard wagon from the back of the barn. They'd harnessed up a four-horse team to pull the wagon. They drove it right past Clint Thacker's body.

The man who'd brained Roy Bennett now grabbed him by the ankles and dragged him outside into the yard in front of the relay station. He lifted the man's hair, making a quick job of it. Unpleasant, but necessary.

The others, and there were more of them now, all wearing clothes similar to each other, pitched in as they wrapped ropes around the big safe inside the relay station and, using their horses, dragged the thing out into the yard. They used some stout boards as a ramp and managed to get the safe up onto the back of the buckboard. It was not easy work, the safe being heavy and awkward, but brute force did the trick. With the safe loaded and tied into place, most of the men mounted their horses and followed the wagon up a long road that wound its way through the mountains. Not a road, really, more like a dirt trail. No one really took it much because it didn't go anywhere except higher and deeper into the mountains. Ultimately, the trail ended at a creek where some gold was found, but that claim panned out in a hurry. There still existed a half dozen weather beaten cabins up where they'd found the gold.

Four of the men stayed back, though. They went to work inside the relay station, breaking up furniture and tossing around clothes and sheets and anything else they could find, and then they set the materials ablaze. Several little fires growing bigger, growing together.

Then they waited. Maybe a quarter of an hour or a little more, until the stagecoach from Silver City, bound for Albuquerque, appeared on the hill above the relay station. The driver saw the smoke rising up from the relay station and jerked his team to a halt. At that, the four men mounted and pushed their horses to a fast gallop, tearing down the main road, ignoring the trail into the mountains that the others with the wagon had taken.

Even if none of the stagecoach passengers saw them, surely the driver and shotgun rider did.

- 2 -

Lucy Blake stepped into the dining room at R. H. Greenleaf's Restaurant and looked around the place for the Wells Fargo man. She spotted him sitting alone in a back corner, his back against the wall and his eye on the front of the restaurant. Most everyone in Greenleaf's turned to look at Lucy Blake. She was a striking figure, tall with a narrow frame, black hair and a pale complexion. But it was not her physical appearance alone that turned heads. Lucy Blake was something of a local celebrity in New Albuquerque – the female Pinkerton detective who had recently been engaged in a gunfight with road agents.

She bore a pink scar across her cheek. The scar started just above the corner of her mouth and ran under the eye patch that covered her injured eye. The Pinkertons sent a doctor from Baltimore, but he'd declared her eye permanently damaged.

It was a shame, as far as Calvin Hughes was concerned. She'd had the prettiest pair of hazel eyes a woman could want.

She strode across the dining room like she owned the place, and all eyes followed her. In spite of himself, Hughes watched her, too.

"May I join you, Mr. Hughes?" Lucy asked.

"Of course, Miss Blake. I'd be hurt if you did not."

She slid out a chair beside him, so that they were both sitting with their backs to the wall and facing out at the dining room.

"I assume you'll be headed south tomorrow?" Lucy said.

Hughes raised his eyebrows.

"What do I not know?" he asked.

He'd grown accustomed in these recent weeks to Lucy Blake knowing just about everything before he did. The Pinkertons claimed that they never slept, and Hughes was beginning to believe it.

Lucy frowned at him as she took his fork from his plate. She stabbed a piece of steak and ate it. Hughes waited while she chewed. It was his first bite. He hadn't even tasted the steak yet.

"I'm famished," she said, only the slightest tone of

apology in her voice.

"What do I not know?" Hughes asked again.

"The Wells Fargo relay station outside of Santa Rita was burned yesterday," Lucy said, casting her good eye on him. "I'm surprised you did not know."

Hughes twisted his lips in frustration. For weeks, Lucy Blake had been taunting him because she was first to know everything, and she had taken to making the constant claim, "I'm surprised you did not know." She enjoyed pursuing a rivalry between the Pinkertons and Wells Fargo, though to Hughes no such rivalry existed. They were both private lawmen, but their respective companies could not be more different. The Pinkertons worked for the highest bidder, but a Wells Fargo man worked for Wells Fargo only.

"The Santa Rita relay station burned?" Hughes said.

"I received a telegram this afternoon," Lucy said. "We've been hired by a copper mining company out of Santa Rita."

Hughes narrowed his eyes.

"Why would a copper mining company hire the Pinkertons to look into a fire at a Wells Fargo relay station?"

Lucy giggled a little as she took another bite from Hughes' plate. That was fine, though. He'd lost his appetite.

She chewed the steak and then she reached across him and slid the plate toward her, along with his knife, and she cut several more bites. Now she talked while she ate. Hughes took a sip of his beer.

"The relay station is not far from the mining company," she said. "So the mining company used the Wells Fargo safe at the relay station – like a bank."

In his mind, Hughes walked the trail of events.

"That doesn't explain the mining company hiring the Pinkertons," he said.

"Oh, yes it does," Lucy Blake said knowingly, and then laughing around the bites of steak in her mouth.

The woman he'd first met on a train bound from Denver to Albuquerque had been a demure pianist, innocent, almost lamb-like the way she was so out of place on the frontier.

But Hughes had learned over the past couple of months, as both of them set up shop in the railroad boomtown for their respective masters, that the demure pianist was an act, a cover for the real woman. She was a tough-as-nails Pinkerton with a ribald sense of humor, and she wore her eye patch and the scar across her cheek like a badge of courage.

Lucy had now completely taken over Hughes' dinner, so he waved at the waiter to get another plate of steak and fried potatoes and green beans. R. H. Greenleaf's put out the best spread in town, and he could only watch Lucy Blake for so long before his appetite returned.

"I'm riding down," Lucy said. "I've hired a wagon and a two-horse team. If you're inclined, you're welcome to come along with me."

"Where is Santa Rita?" Hughes asked.

He was still trying to get acclimated to New Mexico, and while he had an adequate map of the territory in his mind, it did not include every little village.

"You know Santa Rita," Lucy said darkly.

"Do I?"

Lucy nodded. "It's south, on the cutoff to Silver City, up in the mountains."

Calvin Hughes nodded, remembering now.

"The site of the massacre," he said.

"That's the one," Lucy Blake said.

Together, they had worked to learn some about the territory they now called home, and they'd come across a story not long ago of a massacre at Santa Rita. In the 1830s, a white man seeking to earn money from the Mexican government arranged a large feast at the copper mines at Santa Rita. He invited some number of Apache and then slaughtered them, taking the scalps to sell to the Mexican government. Predictably, the massacre enraged the Apache who in turn killed as many as three hundred miners who were fleeing Santa Rita. The mines were a constant site of Apache raids and were closed for many years, though after Cochise signed the peace treaty in '73, the mines at Santa Rita were reopened. Even so, it was a site of occasional Apache raids still today.

"Was it Apache?" Hughes asked.

"It appears so," Lucy said. "Stagecoach driver got a clear look at them riding away."

"Not much for a Pinkerton to do," Hughes said. "Or a Wells Fargo agent, for that matter. I would think the local sheriff would form up a posse. Don't they have a cavalry down there?"

Lucy nodded.

"Troopers from Fort Bayard and maybe some locals formed up a posse. And they've gone looking for the renegades who burned the relay station."

Hughes was certain there was something Lucy Blake was not telling him.

"So why are the Pinkertons involved?" he asked.

Lucy smiled.

"I hesitate to say any more," she said. "If you decide to come with me, you'll find out all you need to know."

The waiter set a plate down in front of Hughes, and together the two of them ate. Their conversation shifted to local gossip. The newly appointed marshal of Albuquerque, Milt Yarberry, was dining at a table not far away. Yarberry, whom Hughes suspected of being an outlaw in a past life, seemed to always be a great source of the town's gossip. Yarberry walked a narrow line, attempting to keep the town respectable on behalf of the town fathers who hired him and not bringing disrepute on the town himself for shooting ne'er-do-wells. The latter came naturally to him.

Hughes wondered, as he did almost every time he saw Milt Yarberry, how long it would be before he and the town marshal had a falling out.

"Are you taking Albert Fears with you?" Hughes said.

"Of course," Lucy said.

That was another one who worried Hughes. Albert Fears turned up in town three weeks ago, sent from Chicago as a second man in the Albuquerque Pinkerton office. Up to then, the Pinkerton office in Albuquerque had been a one-woman show. After Lucy Blake, a Pinkerton detective out of Denver, helped to solve a stagecoach robbery, the Pinkertons made her a detective.

Albert Fears wasn't much of a detective. He

admitted that much himself. But he stood six-foot-three and weighed north of two-fifty. Under his coat he toted a double-barrel shotgun, with the barrel sawed short and the butt removed so that he gripped it like a pistol. Fears would tell you himself: He was muscle, the brawn to Lucy Blake's brains. The Pinkerton company rewarded her for a job well-done by making her the de facto chief of its Albuquerque office and giving her a strongman to add weight to her authority.

So far, they'd found nothing to occupy their time.

Not that Hughes had done much, either.

Most of his work so far in Albuquerque – excepting the initial stagecoach robbery that first brought him to New Mexico – had been administrative work. He'd worked out the costs of his office, put together a budget that included travel expenses for cases in other parts of the state. The biggest thing he'd managed so far was a trip to Las Vegas where he discovered a missing five hundred dollars was down to an accounting error.

For a man who'd made his reputation and career on gunfights with gangs of California outlaws, Calvin Hughes was beginning to get bored in Albuquerque.

"I'll ride along to Santa Rita," he said. "I expect by the time I get back to the office I'll know that the decision isn't mine, anyway."

***

The Western Union telegram on his desk at the Wells, Fargo & Company office in Albuquerque came from James Hume, the head of the company's investigative agency and Calvin Hughes' mentor in California.

Two words stuck out to him in the telegram: "Safe missing."

Hughes put the telegram in his desk drawer and looked across the office to Silas Evans.

"What would a band of Apache off the reservation want with a Wells Fargo safe?" he said.

Silas Evans ran the Wells Fargo Express office. That meant he kept the books, arranged the shipments, managed the company's banking business in Albuquerque, and sold tickets for the stagecoach. He did a little bit of everything, as every Wells Fargo Express man did. He was not, though, much of an investigator, and his interests did not run in that vein.

"I suppose they would want the safe for the same reason anyone else would want it," Silas said absently, his spectacles pinched to his nose and his nose deep inside one of his accounting books.

"And why is that?" Hughes asked.

"For the money inside."

Hughes stretched in his chair and shook his head.

"Apache don't care anything about money," Hughes said.

"Maybe they care for what money can buy," Silas said reasonably. "The value of money is not inherent. The value of money is what other people are willing to trade for it."

"Guns," Hughes said. "Guns and ammunition. That's about the only thing a band of raiding Apache would want that money could get them."

"There you have it," Silas said, clearly intending that to be an end to the conversation.

"Maybe," Hughes said.

The Sandia Mountains east of Albuquerque, visible during the day from Hughes' desk, had disappeared with the fall of the night. All he could see at present through his office window was the depot across Railroad Avenue, currently lit up with lamps inside and out, and the boardwalk that ran, more or less, all the way along New Albuquerque's lone street.

Hughes had seen plenty of boomtowns come and go – the sudden rush of prospectors looking to strike it rich when someone, somewhere, found gold in the bed of a river. But this was a railroad boomtown, and it had a sense of permanence. Nothing had been here a year ago, just a flat stretch of land set between the big river to the west and the Sandia Mountains to the east.

Old Albuquerque, a Spanish mission that had existed for two centuries, had probably always been a place of human habitation. A small collection of adobe buildings centered on a plaza, book-ended by the San Felipe de Neri Church on one end and a rowdy saloon on the other. The Old Town remained active, if not thriving, mostly among those who'd been here long before the engineers for the AT&SF ever started looking for a terminus easier to reach than Santa Fe.

Hughes, so far, felt comfortable in Albuquerque. He enjoyed the promise of a new place. But he'd yet to spend a summer here, and that might prove to be the real test.

"Have you ever yet heard of Apache stealing a safe?" Hughes asked.

Silas Evans frowned and glanced up from his papers, his eyes cresting the top ridge of his spectacles. If a tone of voice could frown, Evans' certainly did now.

"I can't say that I recall hearing of Apache stealing a safe," he said. "But I'm sure there is nothing inherent in the Indian blood that makes him immune from thievery."

Hughes twisted his lips thoughtfully. He stared at Silas Evans without really seeing the man, his thoughts somewhere nearer to Santa Rita and a burned-out Wells Fargo relay station.

"I reckon you'd like to be left to your work," Hughes said.

"I reckon," Silas Evans said.

"Then I'll leave you to it and go have a smoke outside," Hughes said. "I'm riding south tomorrow to see about this business in Santa Rita, so I'll be gone for a few days."

Silas Evans, to demonstrate that theirs was no more than a commercial association, tossed up a hand in farewell without even bidding him a good journey. Hughes smiled at the top of the man's head.

When the cigar rollers in the big cities back east went on strike a couple of years back, demanding better wages, better hours, and some quantity of free cigars each week, the big manufacturers hired out women from the neighborhoods to roll cigars. They discovered quickly that women, with smaller hands and lithe fingers, were superior cigar rollers anyway. In many places, the strikers found themselves permanently unemployed.

Buchanan & Lyall was among the first of the cigar companies to realize that "cigars rolled by a woman's hand" proved itself as a selling phrase, and Calvin Hughes was among those to whom the phrase appealed.

He had a weakness for women, even unseen women in New York City to whom his only connection was that they'd rolled his cigar.

So Hughes became a loyal customer, and it was a Buchanan & Lyall that he now took from the silver three-cigar holder inside his coat.

He swept a match across the rough timber of a wagon parked on the street and drew rapidly on the cigar to get it lit, puffing a cloud of smoke that lit up white and orange in the light of the lamps along the street. As always in the evening, there was a bustle of people on the street in New Albuquerque. Darkness could not conquer the natural desire of these newcomers to mingle.

Though he'd come to Albuquerque under the guise of a road agent looking for a job to pull, Hughes now was widely known in the town for what he truly was. Carrying the name of Wells Fargo made him popular among the merchants who ran the town. They liked being associated with the national reputation of Wells Fargo, and Silas Evans, with his nose in the company ledgers, seldom afforded them the opportunity.

They greeted him as they passed him on the street, stopping to shake hands or make small talk about the chilly breeze or the pretty sunset or the arrival times of the stagecoaches. He found that folks liked to talk to him about stagecoach arrival times quite a bit because it was the one thing everyone knew about the Wells Fargo business. If the stagecoach was late, folks who had no friends nor freight on the coach would still stand on the boardwalk and tap their feet, peering off into the distance for some sign that the stagecoach was on its way. If it was early, folks would hurry behind it along the street to see who might be arriving in town or to get a newspaper or catch some piece of gossip from the world beyond.

Hughes accepted the small talk with a good nature. He was, after all, a representative of Wells, Fargo & Company, and the company paid him well to do work he enjoyed. So he listened to the gossip, talked about the arrival times of the stagecoach, and disabused the notion that trains would one day make the stagecoach obsolete.

"There will always be places the railroad men won't want to go," Hughes would say. "And unless men start growing wings, they'll want Wells and Fargo to take them there."

- 3 -

The big red roan walked with an easy gait, smooth and comfortable on a long ride.

Hughes named the horse Sequoia, and now she mounted a low hill and stood tall at the crest.

"Nothing," Hughes called down to the wagon after surveying the countryside. In almost every direction, some mountain a hundred miles away broke the horizon, but here in the valley along the Rio Grande, where the hard and rocky soil of the desert prevented all but the hardiest of greasewood and mesquite from finding purchase, there was nothing to break the monotony unless he rode down off the road to the bosque that grew only in the narrow footprint of the river's floodplain.

The hill, not more than a few feet high up the easy grade just off the road, seemed to be the tallest spot for miles.

"This is an empty place," Hughes said. "Nothing to recommend it."

The stagecoach made the run from Albuquerque to Silver City in two days of almost non-stop travel. Hughes, Albert Fears, and Lucy Blake were now reaching the end of their second day. They would stop the night at a relay station and in the morning turn west and begin the climb into the mountains. They had one more full day of travel and then most of the next day would get them to Santa Rita.

The temperature was pleasant enough, only the sun's insistence causing beads of sweat to grow on Hughes' forehead. He now slid off his hat and wiped his sleeve across his forehead. Sequoia shifted uneasily on the round top of the small hill, ready to keep going. Even the horse knew this was no place to stay for long.

They'd spent the previous two evenings at relay stations, finding meals and beds gladly offered to a man who carried a Wells Fargo badge and to his companions. To lighten the load on his horse, Hughes had a spare horse he'd let from the livery back in Albuquerque, and he'd ridden that horse the first day and shifted to Sequoia for the second.

While he sat his horse, the wagon rolled past on the road below him. Lucy Blake turning her head sharply to see him with her unpatched eye.

"We wouldn't have made this journey for the sightseeing," she said. "Plenty of other directions of travel offer prettier views."

"It is a wonderment to me that people would even inhabit this place," Hughes replied.

"Not many do," Albert Fears noted.

"No, I suppose not."

"The only people we've encountered so far, occupying this place, are relay station operators in the employ of your company," Lucy Blake noted.

Hughes grunted and touched a leg to the red roan's side. Sequoia came down off the hill and loped out in front of the wagon.

"We'll have prettier views when we cut west," Lucy called ahead to him. "Santa Rita is up in the mountains, and I've heard that Silver City's vistas are lovely."

Though he had no real complaints about Albuquerque, Hughes longed for the high hills along the coast, the lush valley, and the forests of California. He'd found himself several times riding down to the bosque just to be among trees.

Sequoia loped on ahead of the wagon. Even at the end of the day, she kept as strong a pace as she'd had at the start of the day. She was made for these long-distance journeys, and the long, flat road cutting through the desert gave her no challenges that might wear her out.

The trio arrived at the next relay station just a little before dark. The station manager wasn't interested in helping with the horses or in making a supper for his guests, but he gave them free rein in his barn and kitchen. The horses were grateful for the hay, and the Hughes and his companions were satisfied with beans and bacon.

Later, Albert Fears and Lucy Blake joined Hughes on the rocking chairs out front of the adobe relay station.

"I'm glad you came with us," Albert Fears said.

"Why's that?" Hughes asked.

"I reckon I can handle half a dozen road agents at one time, but if we get in a fight with Apache, it'll be good to have another gun beside me. No offense to Miss Blake, but fighting Apache ain't a small thing to consider."

Hughes glanced at Lucy Blake.

"You're settled, then, that it was Apache who burned out the relay station?" Hughes asked Fears.

"The stagecoach driver saw them," Fears said. "I ain't inclined to dispute him."

"No, I suppose not," Hughes said. "But does it not strike you as odd, Mr. Fears, that the Apache made off with a safe?"

Albert Fears shrugged his heavy shoulders and grunted.

"Injuns ain't different from white men," he said. "Some is good, decent folk. Some is ornery thieves."

"I suppose," Hughes mused. "Miss Blake?"

"Mr. Hughes?" Lucy said.

"What are your thoughts?"

Lucy stretched her legs out. She wore a simple blue dress, though Hughes suspect that underneath it she had on pantaloons of some kind. She was always dressed ready for action.

"It does seem strange to me that Apache raiders would trouble themselves with a safe," she said. "Heavy and awkward to transport. And the stage driver did not report seeing a wagon. But until we get to Santa Rita, we don't know much of anything."

"It seems odd to me that the Pinkertons would send a couple of detectives when a posse is already after the Apache," Hughes said.

Lucy smiled, but she did not offer an explanation.

The night air was cool, almost cold. He pinched his coat closed at the neck and pulled the collar up. He nestled his neck down into the collar, more to give warmth to his ears than anything. He was tired from the day's travel, but he knew his mind was not going to leave him alone long enough for sleep to come easy. For the moment, at least, he hoped that Lucy and Albert would continue to sit up with him. Or, in all honesty, he hoped that Albert would turn in and Lucy would continue to sit up with him.

He found that his fondness for her had only grown as he got to know her better. He valued her conversation more than most women he'd known, and despite the scar on her cheek and the eye patch, Hughes found her to be about the prettiest diversion in this desert.

"When we get to Santa Rita, I'll be going directly to the mining company," Lucy said. "You're welcome to come along, if you like."

Hughes drew on his cigar. The evening breeze snatched the smoke away and it disappeared into the night.

"I'll do that," he said. "I'm not sure where else I would start."

The relay station operator, a German man called Buttner, walked out of the station and gave a look down the road.

"Coach from Silver City will arrive soon," he said.

Buttner's son, a boy of about sixteen, assisted him at the station, and he now trotted out to the corral to collect the team to hitch to the coach. The relay station was run as a family operation. Buttner's wife was inside cooking a meal, and his two daughters, younger than the boy, were setting out plates.

"This is a home station, so the passengers will get a meal," Buttner said.

"Might prove useful to hear some news from Silver City," Hughes said.

Buttner wore a permanently stern expression on his face, and he glanced at Hughes like he disagreed with the notion of the Wells Fargo agent talking to the passengers, but then he said, "Yes, I thought so, too. Every coach through here from Silver City has been full of gossip about it."

"What have they said?" Lucy asked.

"They've brought rumors of other Apache raids on small settlements in the mountains," he said. "I do not know if I believe them. Even if I do, I don't know that I believe there have been nearly as many raids as they claim. I do not like all the talk about Apache. It makes my wife and daughters nervous. They think now the Apache will be on us here."

"Have you ever had trouble with Apache here?" Hughes asked.

"Not once. Though one time two years back, a band of Mescalero warriors rode through here. They stopped to water their horses and then moved on. We heard later that they had killed some prospectors near Silver City, but I never thought it was the same band. Those that came here were peaceful enough."

"Do you worry about Indians?" Lucy asked.

Buttner shook his head.

"I worry about road agents," he said. "They can sometimes be cruel to women."

Buttner looked back over his shoulder into the relay station at his two daughters. Then he dropped his voice so he wouldn't be overheard.

"I worry for them. They are pretty girls, and I know what some of those sorts would do the them. But I do not worry about Indians."

Hughes held his cigar a ways away from his face and watched the amber glow for a moment.

"Ever had trouble with road agents?" he asked.

Unless they were stealing horses, it was rare for road agents to bother a relay station. Very few of them ever had much in the way of valuables, and most of the operators were willing to share what they had with travelers, negating the need for violence from men who might be hungry enough to kill for a meal.

"Never have," Buttner said.

Hughes raised his eyebrows at Lucy Blake. Most folks he encountered, especially in the untamed corners, feared Indians. And most of the time they feared them without just cause. Twenty or thirty years ago, Indian attacks were more common in some places. But these days, raiding parties were rare. Buttner was probably right to be more afraid of road agents.

A short while later the stagecoach kicked up a whirlwind of dust in the yard outside the relay station.

As it turned out, the driver and shotgun rider were the ones who'd seen the Apache as they fled the burning Santa Rita station.

"We come up on the relay station, and the first thing I seen was the smoke, even before we topped the hill," said the shotgun rider, a man named Kays. "I says to Billy, 'There's something ablaze up ahead.' I tightened my grip on my gun, I can tell you that, 'cause I figured road agents had set a fire and blocked the road."

"We was too close to the Santa Rita station for that," Billy, the driver, said. "I knew it wasn't going to be road agents."

"Well, I tightened my grip all the same," Kays continued. "Then we come up over the hill above the station, and seen the whole thing ablaze."

Hughes marveled at his good luck of catching the same driver and shotgun rider who'd witnessed the incident. In his years of experience investigating stagecoach robberies, Hughes knew one of the toughest parts of his job was tracking down the drivers and shotgun riders who witnessed holdups because they never stopped running their routes.

They were seated inside the relay station at a table removed from the passengers. Kays and Billy eating their bacon and beans while the passengers ate at a larger table in the middle of the front room. Hughes was standing, leaning against the wall. Lucy Blake sat at the table across from Kays. Albert Fears, though, had used the arrival of the stagecoach as an opportunity to turn in, and Albert had gone to the back room he was sharing with Hughes and Buttner's son.

"The fire was going pretty good?" Hughes asked.

"Oh, hell yes," Kays said, and he glanced at his passengers and said, "Excuse my language."

The passengers, though, were all men, probably from the diggings around Silver City, and Hughes figured it was better than even odds these men had heard and probably uttered far worse.

"Billy jerked the lines and hollered at the team to stop as soon as we seen the fire. I saw Roy Bennett splayed out there in the yard, recognized him from all that distance. Right away I knew it was Roy. I says to Billy, 'Billy – that's Roy there in the yard.'"

"And I says, 'And them's Apache riding off,'" Billy added.

"You saw them?" Hughes said.

"Sure I seen, 'em. That's how we knew they was Apache," Billy said.

"Did you see them too?" Hughes asked Kays.

"I seen 'em," Kays said, and his brow clouded over as he spoke. "No question about it. I think I've run this route long enough to recognize an Apache."

"You've been attacked by Apache?" Hughes asked.

Billy and Kays looked at each other.

"Well, never attacked, but we've seen 'em," Billy

said.

"I did one time have to fire my shotgun when we saw some ahead of us on the road."

"What did they do?" Hughes asked.

"Well, they got off the road," Kays said.

"How many were there?" Hughes asked.

"That time we saw them on the road?" Kays said.

"No. At the Santa Rita station. When you saw it was on fire and you saw the Apache riding away, how many were there?"

Kays rolled both eyes toward the ceiling and squinted hard with one eye as he gave it some thought, counting in his memory.

"Four of them," Kays said.

"And what were they doing?" Hughes asked.

"They was fleeing the scene," Kays said.

"When you saw them, were they already mounted?"

Again, Kays rolled his eyes into his head, trying to picture the moment.

"They wasn't mounted when we first come over the hill," Billy said right away. "I know that for a fact. We seen the smoke and I pulled the lines right away. Then Kays pointed out to me Roy Bennett's body in the yard, and I looked around, and right out there near the barn, just beside the road, I seen the Apache. Four of them, like Kays said, and I clearly remember them looking at us, looking direct at us, and I watched one of 'em slide his foot into the stirrup and swing himself on his horse. The horse was facing east – down the road away from us. But that Apache, he was looking back over his shoulder, direct at us, even as he swung up into the saddle. And then they was gone. Tore off down the road, them horses galloping for all they were worth."

Hughes pursed his lips and glanced at Lucy Blake. If she'd caught anything unusual in the story, she didn't acknowledge it.

"Do you think there were others, or just the four?" Hughes asked.

"The four was all we seen," Kays said.

"And then what?"

"Then we rode down to the station. We found Roy, and Clint. They was dead and scalped, both of them. Dang Injuns scalped 'em both. Might have done worse to the bodies if we hadn't come along."

"Except that they were with their horses and ready to leave when you came over the hill," Hughes said.

"I suppose," Kays said.

"Did you go into the station, to see if there was anyone else inside?" Hughes asked.

Kays rolled up his face like the question was absurd.

"Hell no," he said. "The whole dang place was on fire. A man couldn't have gone into there."

Lucy frowned and she turned to look at Hughes.

"The two men were killed and scalped," she said. "Surely the Apache did that before they set the station on fire."

33

"I would think so, ma'am," Kays said. "Clint was over by the stable, so they probably killed him when he come out to get a team ready for us. Then, because he was out in the yard, we thought they must have jumped Roy Bennett when he come out to see why Clint didn't have the team ready yet. Then we figured they went inside and set the place on fire."

Hughes gave Lucy a grin. She'd picked up one of the pieces in the story that had caught his attention.

"Me and the passengers stayed there at the station," Billy said. "Kays got one of the horses from the stables, saddled it up, and rode to the Santa Rita mine to let them know. Somebody there rode on back to Fort Bayard to raise the alarm."

"I gave all the information we could to the folks at the mine that rode up to the station," Kays said. "Then we changed out the horses ourselves and set on about our way."

"Even though you knew there were Apache on the road in front of you?" Lucy asked.

"Well, sure, ma'am," Billy said. "If they'd meant the stagecoach harm, they'd have attacked us there at the station. And we've got a job to do that don't involve being scared to keep rolling down the road."

- 4 -

Calvin Hughes helped Albert Fears set up the tents within sight of the burned remains of the Santa Rita relay station.

The adobe walls of the station were still largely intact, but the guts of the place were destroyed, and what remained of the roof had caved in. Even days later, the smell of smoke still hung heavy in the small valley where the station had been.

The stable was empty. Someone, presumably from Silver City, had come to get the Wells Fargo horses. But there was plenty of hay, and Hughes and Fears turned out their horses in the corral beside the station barn before they went to work setting up their tents.

As they'd cut west and climbed into the hills, the air got chillier, and Hughes was glad he'd put a canvas tent in the back of the Pinkertons' wagon.

They put up the tents in a clearing between some large juniper bushes. They were not yet quite high enough into the mountains that there were big pines, but the juniper grew tall and fat here, and there were some pinon pines and a few tiny oaks and hardwoods.

"It's too late in the day to try to go down to the mine," Lucy said. "We can do that first thing in the morning."

"Probably also be worthwhile to ride over to Fort Bayard," Hughes said. "It's on the way to Silver City, and I suppose we should plan to check in with the sheriff there."

Hughes and Albert Fears found a stash of firewood back behind where the station had been, far enough away that it hadn't burned up with everything else, and between them they toted enough wood to build a fire and keep it going through the evening. They had in the wagon plenty of provisions for a few days, and before sunset they had a meal of biscuits and bacon and beans cooking on the open fire.

And that's when a dozen uniformed men rode in from the east, coming down into the small valley where the burned-out relay station sat. Buffalo soldiers, led by a white second-lieutenant. Another white man riding with them was not in uniform, and they also rode with an Indian who was not in uniform.

The troopers reined in when they arrived at the site where Hughes and Fears had set up the tents, and the white man who was not in uniform, along with the second lieutenant and one of the Buffalo soldiers who wore a corporal's chevron, rode their horses up near the campsite.

"You've picked a poor place to camp," the white man not in uniform said. "Just a few days back that burned out building was intact and the home of a stagecoach relay station. Apache attacked it and burned it out."

Hughes stood up and stepped away from the fire, sparing himself the indignity of having smoke blow in his face while he spoke to the mounted men.

"We're aware of what happened here. My name is Calvin Hughes. I'm an agent for Wells Fargo."

The white man, the one not in uniform, raised his eyebrows in surprise.

"Huh," he grunted. "I reckon I'm surprised that Wells Fargo would send an investigator for an Indian raid. This is a matter for the army."

Hughes ignored the comment.

"You men from Fort Bayard?" he asked.

"The soldiers are," the man said. "But I'm from Silver City. I'm a deputy sheriff. Dan Tucker is the name."

Tucker squinted a little, watching to see if the Wells Fargo man reacted to his name and was disappointed when he did not. Dangerous Dan Tucker had a reputation, and so he figured the Wells Fargo agent was too new in the territory to have heard of him.

"You ain't been here long?" Tucker said, pulling the reins on his horse as it attempted to get at some tall grass.

"Just set up camp today," Hughes responded.

"No, I mean in the territory," Tucker said.

"A few months," Hughes told him. "We're from Albuquerque."

"Well, Albuquerque, most folks who've been in the territory for a while have heard of Dangerous Dan Tucker," Tucker said of himself.

Hughes wasn't too interested. Back in California they called him "Parlous." Everyone was called by something.

"I've heard the posse was out looking for the Apaches that done this," Hughes said, nodding his head toward the burned-out relay station. "I don't suppose you're that posse?"

"We are," Tucker said.

The horse was determined to get at the grass, and finally Tucker had enough of it. He gave the reins a cruel jerk, and then he swung a leg over and dropped down out of the saddle. He turned loose the reins and let the horse have its snack.

"We tracked the four Apache all the way to the Rio Grande," Tucker said. "They had a jump on us, we reckon by quite a bit. We never did catch up to them, and at the river their tracks scattered."

Hughes looked over at the second lieutenant who had still not introduced himself. He was a young man. He looked barely old enough to be riding in the cavalry, and he had the air of a boy trying to compensate for his age by projecting a gruff attitude.

"Your tracker any good?" Hughes asked him.

"He can track Apache," the second lieutenant said.

"What's your plan next?" Hughes said, leaving the question open for either man to answer.

Tucker turned to the second lieutenant.

"What's the plan, lieutenant?" he said.

"We're going back to the fort," the lieutenant answered. "If there are further reports of Apache in the area, we'll respond to that. But if we can't track them, we can't catch them. For all we know, they've made it to Mexico by now."

Hughes wasn't surprised. Posses, whether they were a ragtag band of local citizens or a company of cavalrymen, typically lasted right up to the first obstacle and then they had a way of losing all their steam. Hughes had ridden once with a posse of sheriff's deputies, bankers, and farmers – two dozen men in all – and as soon as the road agents they were chasing shot one man out of his saddle in an ambush, everyone else gave up and went home. He'd heard of a posse once that reached a river and, failing to find a ford, gave up and turned around. A gang of road agents that was willing to ride far and fast enough could often be guaranteed of getting away. And then it would fall to the wanted posters to catch them, and that could take years. Or maybe never.

"And you?" he asked Tucker.

Tucker shrugged.

"Hell, if this was a band of road agents, I'd chase them clear to the Atlantic, but the Apache are the army's problem. If the army is done, I'm done, too."

"What about the safe?" Lucy Blake asked. She'd

been silent the whole time, letting Hughes talk to the army man and the deputy sheriff.

"And who are you, miss?" Tucker asked.

"My name is Lucy Blake," she said. "I am a detective with the Pinkerton Detective Agency."

"A Pinkerton?" Tucker asked, glancing at Hughes. Hughes nodded his head to confirm Lucy Blake's employment. Tucker sighed, as if he was slightly embarrassed to have to answer the woman. "Ma'am, someone said a safe was missing, but we don't know that for sure. Personally, I don't know that there ever was a safe in this relay station, or if there was one at one time, if it was still there the day the Apache burned this place and killed those two men. All I know for sure is that four Apache were seen leaving this relay station, the two station operators was dead and scalped, and the relay station itself was set ablaze. We tracked them Indians as far as we could, all the way down to the Rio Grande, and they got away from us. As to a safe or what might have happened to a safe, those are all things I don't know about."

Lucy turned her head slightly so that her one good eye was boring into the deputy sheriff, and Dangerous Dan Tucker shifted uneasily to fall under her glare.

Hughes had taken a step away, leaving Lucy Blake free to work. He enjoyed watching her generally, but specifically it was interesting to see her interrogate a deputy sheriff in this way.

"Deputy Tucker, I can assure you there are people paying good money to have me here because of the valuables located within that safe," Lucy said. "So there most certainly was a safe here. Now do you think four mounted Apache rode away with that safe?"

Tucker shook his head.

"No, ma'am, I do not," he said. "But we know it was Apache that done this. And we know which way they rode off. And we know they didn't have a safe strapped onto their backs. You say there was a safe, but I don't know that there was. I can only work with what I know."

Lucy continued her accusatory tone, as if she was interrogating a suspect rather than chatting with a colleague. Tucker had treated her in a dismissive way, patronizing in his tone, and Hughes could hardly blame Miss Blake if she was irked.

"Deputy, you cannot simply dismiss the existence of the safe because you did not personally see it," Lucy said. "Surely your position as a lawman demands that you would at least make some small investigation into the notion that a safe is missing."

Tucker took a big breath and let out in frustration.

"Ma'am, Apache don't care nothing about a safe. If there was a safe here, and if it ain't here now, them Apache didn't have nothing to do with that."

"So you think the safe was removed by someone else before the Apache attacked this relay station?" Lucy said.

Tucker shrugged his shoulders.

"That makes more sense than Apache on horseback riding away with a safe."

Tucker offered an apologetic grin to Hughes as he snatched up the reins of the horse and pulled it back towards him so that he could remount. He tightened the cinch before stepping into the stirrup. Maybe it was sympathetic grin, one man feeling sorry for another who had to endure an overbearing woman.

"If you need anything, Albuquerque, I'm in Silver City. Always happy to lend a hand to the Wells Fargo folks. I wouldn't advise staying here too long. Whether its Apache or someone else, there's all kinds of bad sorts roaming these mountains, and y'all have the look of easy prey."

And that was it. The second-lieutenant called to his men, and the troopers turned their mounts and loped on up the hill to the west, heading home.

Hughes and Albert Fears went back to cooking their supper.

- 5 -

"The first thing I did was send a telegram to St. Louis to let them know the safe was gone," Cushman said.

He was a stout man, short and heavy, but he had a pair of powerful arms and a barrel chest, and on his face, he wore a thick beard that probably was the result of too much time without access to a good razor.

Cushman worked out of a walled canvas tent that overlooked the mining operation. There were about a hundred men living in tents and digging into the hillside. On the ride to the mining operation, as they descended down into the valley and up the other side to Cushman's office, Hughes counted more than a dozen tunnel entrances. Probably all of them connected at least to one or two other tunnels.

They found Cushman in his tent in a heated argument with another man. They stayed back a respectful distance, though Hughes tried to hear what the two were arguing about. But as soon as Cushman saw them, he dropped the conversation with the others.

"Who the hell are you?" Cushman demanded of them.

Hughes swung out of the saddle and Lucy Blake stepped down off the wagon. Albert Fears kept his seat, the lines draped across his lap and the wagon brake on.

"I'm Lucille Blake. I'm a detective with the Pinkerton Detective Agency. We've been hired by the Gibbons and White Mining Company, and I'm looking for Mr. Cushman."

"The Pinkertons? It's about time. I'm Cushman," the stout, bearded man said. "Gibbons and White owns this mining operation. I manage the site."

The other man left the tent without another word. Hughes watched him go. Like Cushman, he was a man with a powerful build, though taller.

"That looked like an angry conversation," Lucy said when the man had walked away. "Is everything all right?"

Cushman sighed heavily.

"No. Everything is not all right. I've got a hundred diggers who are waiting to get paid, and I've got no money to pay them."

He looked angrily from Hughes to Lucy.

"What do you want?"

"We were hired to look into the incident at the relay station," Lucy said.

"I know what you were hired for," Cushman said.

And that's where Cushman started his story.

He pulled together a couple of camp chairs into a patch of morning sunlight falling around the tall juniper bushes, and the three of them sat down in the sun in front of Cushman's tent. He went through the whole thing from his perspective. A mounted man – it turned out to be Kays, the shotgun rider from the stagecoach – road into the mining camp raising the alarm about an Apache attack on the Santa Rita relay station. Cushman saddled a horse and rode with Kays back to the station while sending a couple of men to Fort Bayard to raise the alarm.

"Place was burning good by the time I got there, and there wasn't a thing that could be done about it," Cushman said. "Just had to let it burn out. The men from the stagecoach, Kays and Billy, well, I know them. So they told me everything they'd seen. How they'd come over the hill and seen them Apache riding off. Then they left. Hitched a new team and went. I waited with a couple of my men from the mine, and then when the soldiers arrived, I told them all I knew."

Cushman couldn't say how, but word reached Silver City, and before the soldiers had gone in pursuit of the Apache, Dan Tucker and another deputy sheriff turned up. Tucker said he'd ride with the posse and the other deputy went back to Silver City.

In the meantime, the fire had pretty well burned out, and the soldiers and some of Cushman's men took shovels and pickaxes and began going through the burned-out structure.

Cushman was the first to realize the safe was gone.

"I used that safe at the relay station because I don't have any kind of safe here," he said. "I've used it for two years. The payroll comes in on the stagecoach every month, and Roy Bennett, he's the operator at the station – or was, I guess. Roy just puts it in the safe until I come up to get it."

"You always go to get the payroll or do you send someone else?" Hughes asked.

"I do," Cushman said. "I take the two Pinkerton boys here, you know, as a precaution."

"Two Pinkerton boys?" Lucy asked.

"Sure," Cushman said. "We have two Pinkertons on site here. Didn't you know?"

"No," Lucy said.

"They make sure we don't have problems with the workers – you understand – and do things like guard the payroll when I ride up to the station to fetch it."

"Where are they now?" Lucy asked.

"They went with the posse to follow them Apache."

Lucy cut her eyes at Calvin Hughes, who returned the look. It was interesting to Hughes that Lucy was unaware that there were Pinkertons already on site, and both of them were curious why the Pinkertons had not been with the returning posse the previous evening.

"How much is the payroll?" Lucy asked.

"Thirty-five hundred," Cushman said. "But

sometimes it's double that. Sometimes they run late, so they send two months at one time. This time there were two months payroll at the relay station. I hadn't been to get it yet, even though it had been there for a couple of days."

Hughes again glanced at Lucy. She cut her eye back at him. In the look that passed between them, there was agreement that the Apache got very lucky to have double the usual payroll in the safe.

"Why would you not have gone to get it?" Hughes asked. "Weren't the men already late getting at least half their pay?"

"Yep," Cushman said. "About two weeks late getting their pay for the previous month. But most of these men have worked for me here for several months. They know they'll get paid, and nobody worries much if it's a week or two late. But now there's no payroll, and some of these fellers here are fit to be tied. And them Pinkerton boys are still off with the posse. The first thing I did was send a telegram to St. Louis to let them know the safe was gone."

"They'll replace the payroll?" Hughes asked.

Cushman shrugged.

"Eventually, I reckon they will. They told me to manage the situation. But how the hell am I supposed to manage a hundred men who haven't been paid for a month and probably ain't getting paid this month, neither?"

"How long have you been the foreman here?" Lucy asked.

"I've been here almost two years, and before this is all over, I'll probably be out of a job."

"Why would they dismiss you?" Lucy asked.

"I'm the man caught in the middle," he said. "I've got all these diggers expecting to get paid. I've got Gibbons and White that's already out seven thousand and not real high on the idea of spending another seven thousand. I can see what's going on here. They've hired you to recover the money because they don't want to cough up another seven thousand to pay these men. In a week, they'll fire me and send in someone new to soothe the angry diggers. About the only hope I have now of keeping my job is if you can catch them Apache."

Cushman looked doubtfully from Hughes to Lucy.

"You look like the worst two Indian fighters I ever seen," he said. Then he added lamely, "No offense."

"Who knows that the relay station safe is where you keep the payroll?" Lucy asked.

Cushman shrugged.

"It ain't a secret. I reckon everyone here knows I ride up to the relay station and come back with the payroll."

"Who knows, other than you, that there were two payrolls in that safe?" Hughes asked.

Cushman laughed.

"A hundred diggers at this camp. They all know they haven't been paid in a month. Now, they couldn't know when the payroll would show up there, but they could any one of them figure out that two months' worth of pay was going to be there. But none of that matters. Them Apache wouldn't know, and they're the ones who took it."

"Anybody outside of this camp know about your arrangement to keep the payroll in the Wells Fargo safe?" Hughes asked.

Cushman shrugged.

"Maybe. There's other folks besides me that used that safe. Roy Bennett ran all that, and who knows what he might have mentioned to someone? You're not thinking someone else did this, other than the Apaches?"

"Anything is possible," Hughes said.

.

- 6 -

The three investigators left the Gibbons and White mine and continued west on the road toward Fort Bayard. They moved at an easy pace, Hughes riding along on the red roan beside the wagon.

"What do you think?" Lucy asked when they were a short ways along the road and away from the mine.

"I think Cushman is a man who is feeling some strain," Hughes said.

"Yes. He's probably correct that he'll be fired. It'll be easy for Gibbons and White to send a new foreman to promise everyone that they'll be paid and that the man whose poor decisions led to the loss of the payroll has been replaced."

"I'm guessing the accounting books are all burned up," Hughes said. "Or else they were in the safe. But it would be interesting to know who else was using the safe."

Lucy turned her head to look at him with her good eye.

"What are you thinking?" she said.

Hughes twisted in the saddle and grinned at her.

"What are you thinking?" he responded.

Lucy leaned back while Albert Fears kept his eyes on the road in front of them. She grinned through a moment of silence.

"I'm thinking that you and I are falling into a professional rivalry," she said.

Hughes laughed, and he gave a little leg to Sequoia.

"We may be," he said. "And with that in mind, I'm going to ride on ahead. I'll see you back at the campsite later?"

Lucy Blake squinted her eye and pursed her lips into a vicious frown.

"If it's going to be a competition, we should put a wager on it," she said.

"Whichever of us recovers the money has to take the other to dinner," Hughes suggested.

"That hardly seems like a worthwhile wager," Lucy pouted, and Hughes was glad to see she was taking his intention to ride ahead in good spirit. He wasn't sure initially that she would. The professional rivalry existed long before either of them admitted to it.

"Why is it not fair?" Hughes asked.

"You take me to dinner on a regular basis," Lucy said. "When I win our wager, it won't hardly seem like I've won anything."

Hughes grinned at her.

"Ante up, then," Hughes said. "Name your stake."

Lucy Blake rolled her eye toward the sky and touched an index finger to the corner of her mouth, striking a thoughtful pose. And then she grinned mischievously. Hughes had come to realize she was a terribly playful flirt, and he rather liked it.

"What about a picnic?" she said. "Down by the river, under the willow trees and cottonwoods. But not until spring, when it's pretty out."

"All right, Lucy Blake, it's a bet. If you recover that money, I'll take you and Mr. Fears down to the river for a picnic come springtime."

Albert Fears chuckled heartily at being included in the wager and tipped his hat at Hughes.

"However, if I recover the money, regardless of who receives the credit in the newspapers, then you'll take me to dinner at Greenleaf's, and Mr. Fears can stay at home."

Fears laughed all the harder now.

"I look forward to our picnic," Fears said.

The red roan galloped on ahead of the wagon. Hughes did not think of himself as especially competitive.

Wells Fargo did not care for the glory of solving a case or for getting in headlines in newspapers. James Hume, Hughes' mentor and boss, did not care how a mystery was solved or who received credit for putting road agents in prison. Yet still, Hughes wanted to be sure that he was the one who recovered the money, even if Lucy Blake and the Pinkerton Detective Agency received the credit.

Hughes rode through the rolling hills that grew farther up into the Mogollon Mountains. Mountain peaks to the north and east gave him a sense of the nearby highlands. The area was dotted with juniper, and good grass, unlike the desert they'd come through down along the Rio Grande, but he was still not yet high enough to be among the tall pines that would provide good shade for a traveler. The sun's constant presence in the late morning meant that Hughes was sweating under his coat and canvas duster, but the chilly wind prevented him from removing the coat, and knowing what the trail dust would do to his good clothes, he kept the duster on him.

Fort Bayard sat on the road between the Santa Rita mine and Silver City, and the road was well-traveled, mostly level, and an easy stroll for horse and rider. Sequoia managed it at a steady lope, and Hughes quickly outdistanced the buckboard wagon.

The road dipped down into a dry wash. The creek bed was flat and wide, and Hughes figured it probably ran pretty good in the wet season. The banks were crowded with cottonwoods, all bare of leaves now, and little willows and scrub trees. The buildings of Fort Bayard were just beyond the dry wash, about a mile away.

The barracks and quartermaster's stores were all long, row buildings, a single story. But like most forts out

West, the officers were quartered in large, two-story buildings with grand porches and balconies. All the buildings shone bright white in the sun, the red roof tiles absolutely glowing above the blinding white buildings. From a distance, the fort seemed clean and crisp.

As he approached, Hughes could see several soldiers performing drills on the open parade ground. Though there'd raged plenty of debate back east about the usefulness of colored troopers, any man who spent much time in the West could quickly vouch for them, especially in those areas disturbed by Indians off the reservations. The Buffalo soldiers were as feared among the Apache as the Apache were feared among the settlers.

Hughes rode directly toward the building he'd decided was likely the officers' quarters. There were two large buildings, almost identical. Hughes guess that one was likely a fort hospital. But the other one had several men in uniform sitting in rockers on the front porch. As he neared the building, he came upon a group of about a dozen soldiers. When he was even with them, he recognized one among them as the corporal who'd been with the posse the day before. Hughes settled back in the saddle, and Sequoia came to an abrupt stop.

"That's a fine horse," the corporal said, and even as he spoke his eyes moved over the red roan. "I was admiring her coming down off of that hill. Good gait, strong haunches, prominent withers."

"She's a good horse," Hughes agreed. "A little ornery at times."

The corporal laughed.

"She's a red, so that's what you would expect."

Hughes already had in mind what he wanted, and it occurred to him he was more likely to get it from a corporal than any officer.

"What's your name, Corporal?" Hughes asked.

"Greaves, sir."

"Do you remember me, Corporal Greaves? I spoke briefly to your lieutenant yesterday at the relay station."

"I remember," the man said. "You're the Wells Fargo man."

"That Indian guide that was with you yesterday, is he around here somewhere? I'd like to talk to him."

Greaves turned and looked toward the small collection of buildings that constituted the town, about two hundred yards from the fort.

"You see that third building from the right down yonder?" Greaves asked. "That's the Wet Whistle Saloon, and that's where you'd find him about this time of day."

Hughes frowned.

"A bit early to be drinking," he said.

Corporal Greaves shrugged.

"Maybe for you, but not for him."

"He have a name?" Hughes asked, doubting that he would recognize the man.

"His name is Yuyutsu, but everyone calls him Apache Tom."

Hughes nodded and started to pick up the reins, but Greaves stopped him.

"What do you want with him?"

"I want to ask him about those men you were tracking," Hughes said.

Corporal Greaves shook his head.

"Won't do you any good. He won't talk to you. I'll talk to you, though."

Hughes stood in his stirrup and swung a leg over the back of Sequoia. He loosened the girth on the saddle and dropped the reins to the ground to keep Sequoia from wandering far. The other men who'd been standing with the corporal now all wandered away. Hughes thought the corporal must have sent them away with a look.

"What can you tell me?" Hughes asked.

"It's like the lieutenant and the deputy said yesterday. We followed those tracks all the way down to the Rio Grande. The tracks split up, and we chased them one way and then another. They went down into the river, went a mile upstream, crossed, and then went back in the river and went a half mile downstream. And that's where we lost them for good and the lieutenant decided to come on back."

Hughes frowned. He'd hoped for something a little more.

"How long have you been fighting Apache, Corporal Greaves?"

"Oh, I reckon five or six years now," Greaves said.

"You ever see Apache ride with a saddle?" Hughes asked.

Greaves chuckled.

"I reckon I never have," he said.

Hughes nodded thoughtfully, giving Corporal Greaves an opportunity to elaborate or ask a question of his own. But he didn't volunteer anything more.

"Those men you followed, did they ride like Apache you've encountered before?" Hughes asked.

Greaves narrowed his eyes.

"Well, we never saw them, so I don't know that I can give an opinion on how they rode."

"I mean following their tracks – going upstream and downstream and all that – did they use Apache tricks to try to confuse you?"

Corporal Greaves nodded.

"If that's what you mean, then I reckon I'd say yes. Losing their tracks in a river like that, that's definitely a thing Apache will do. But most road agents would do that, too. Or soldiers, for that matter. It's not like those are tricks only Apache understand."

Hughes decided to try the same question from a different way.

"Was there anything that made you think maybe they weren't Apache?" he asked.

"The men on the stagecoach said they saw Apache riding away," Greaves said.

Hughes rubbed his chin thoughtfully and chewed his lip for a moment. Then he reached into his coat and took out a silver cigar case and snapped it open. There were three cigars inside. He removed two and held one out to Corporal Greaves. Hughes struck a match and lit his cigar, and the corporal also lit his.

"Not a bad cigar," Corporal Greaves said, taking another draw. "I'm obliged to you."

"It's a good cigar," Hughes said. "Rolled by women in New York City."

"Is that right?" Greaves asked.

"That's what it says on the label, anyway," Hughes said. "I know what the stagecoach men said they saw. I talked to them a couple of days back. But now I'm asking you what you saw."

Corporal Greaves smiled. He looked over one shoulder and then the other to be sure their conversation was not being overheard.

"You didn't hear this from me," he said. "But I can tell you for a fact that those weren't Apache, and any man who rode in that posse could tell you the same."

"Even though you never saw them?" Hughes asked, skeptically.

"Yes, sir."

"How do you know for certain?"

Greaves smiled broadly.

"Because Apache don't ride shod horses. These was definitely not Apache. Mexicans, maybe. White men, probably. Could've even been Negroes. But not Apache."

"And the Indian scout in the Whistle Stop Saloon, he'd say the same thing?" Hughes asked.

"It's the Wet Whistle Saloon, and I don't know what he would say. But it don't matter what he says. Them horses we tracked wasn't rid by Apache."

As they talked, a white officer stepped down from the porch of the building Hughes figured to be the officer's quarters. He walked several steps across the yard and then shouted.

"Corporal Greaves! Do you not have duties to tend to?" the man shouted.

"Is that the lieutenant I met yesterday?" Hughes asked.

"That's him," Greaves said, and the frown creeping across his face suggested he was not particularly fond of the lieutenant.

Greaves took a step away from Hughes and turned toward the officer.

"Yes, sir," Greaves shouted. "Getting to it just now, sir."

But Greaves turned back to Hughes, taking a draw on the cigar.

"I don't want to get you in trouble," Hughes said.

"Won't be no trouble," Greaves said. "I've learned a long time ago that if I get a bad lieutenant, I just need to wait him out. They all leave soon enough. The good ones get promoted and go back East. The bad ones leave the army, either by choice or by force. And the really bad ones get sent down to the border to deal with cattle rustlers coming across the river. This particular lieutenant will be gone in four days."

"Is he headed to the border?" Hughes asked.

Greaves laughed.

"I could wish," he said. "This one is mustering out."

"And he's the same lieutenant that rode with the posse?" Hughes asked, just to be certain.

"Same one."

"He didn't decide to end the chase so that he could be back to the fort in time to muster out, did he?"

Greaves squinted at Hughes.

"I wouldn't put that past him, but we lost the trail at the river. There was no point in continuing."

"Corporal Greaves!" the lieutenant shouted once again from across the yard, taking a few more steps toward Hughes and the corporal.

"I should be getting on," Greaves said.

Hughes gave a touch to the brim of his hat, and the corporal went on about his business. Hughes decided he was not interested in talking to the lieutenant. He checked the cinch on his saddle

***

"That's an interesting observation," Dan Tucker said.

"Are you disputing it?" Calvin Hughes asked him.

"Not at all," Deputy Tucker said grinning. "I will corroborate for you that the tracks we followed were those of horses wearing shoes. In fact, I made the same observation in my report to Sheriff Whitehill. But it is an interesting observation, all the same."

"What does it tell you?" Hughes asked.

"Could be that the Apache stole those horses out of

the corral," Tucker said. "The men on the stagecoach said they saw Apache, and I wasn't in a position to dispute what they saw. So the simple explanation is that the Apache renegades attacked the relay station and stole some shod horses to get away."

"I'm not convinced of that," Hughes said. "What's the harder explanation?"

Tucker chewed his lip. Hughes found the deputy sheriff standing on the boardwalk out front of a saloon on a busy street in downtown Silver City. Tucker was leaning against a post and scowling at all the coming and going on the street. Part of being a deputy sheriff in a prospecting boomtown, which Silver City certainly still was, involved leaning against things and attempting to intimidate. Dangerous Dan Tucker, whatever other qualities he had as a lawman, certainly had that part down.

Following his conversation with Corporal Greaves, Hughes decided not to linger at the Fort Bayard. If it turned out that these men were not Apache, the murders at the relay station were not an Army matter. Instead, they would prove to be a matter for the local lawmen, and he wanted to talk to Dangerous Dan Tucker before Lucy Blake and Albert Fears got to him.

"The harder explanation is that someone went to some trouble to fool the stagecoach men into blaming the Apache," Tucker said. "That's a harder explanation."

Hughes nodded.

"And what would you say to me if I told you that is the explanation I'm leaning toward."

Tucker shrugged.

"That's your business, Mr. Wells Fargo," Tucker said.

"You ask me about a safe, and I don't know if that safe was even there. You ask me about shod horses, and I can tell you a good reason why Apache might have been riding on shod horses. Unless I have something more, I don't know what I'm supposed to do about it."

"Would the Apache take a safe?" Hughes asked. He'd already asked the deputy about the safe once, but Tucker shrugged it off the first time he asked.

"No," Tucker said. "I'll say for certain that the Apache didn't take a safe."

"So if you had to guess, who would you say took it?" Hughes asked.

The ride from Fort Bayard to Silver City had taken longer than Hughes expected it would, and it was coming onto mid-afternoon now. He would have to a tough time making it back to his camp beyond Santa Rita before dark.

Dan Tucker shook his head slowly.

"I can't say. I mean, I didn't even know until someone at the Gibbons and White mine mentioned it that they even kept a safe there," Tucker said. "Do you have a safe at every relay station? It's just not something I knew about. And if I didn't know, then who did? I reckon the first place you would start is by figuring out who knew that there was a safe up there worth taking. Cushman, the foreman at the mine, I think he's the one that told me about the safe."

Hughes nodded.

"What happened to the horses that were at the relay station?" Hughes asked.

Tucker shrugged.

"Couldn't tell you. I was riding with the posse. When

I left, the corral was full. When we come back yesterday, the corral was empty – except for your horses."

Hughes had to wonder about Dan Tucker. He seemed, at best, disinterested in the possibility that a safe had been stolen from the Wells Fargo relay station.

"What do you intend to do next about it?" Hughes asked.

Tucker shook his head and sucked his teeth noisily.

"I reckon, unless some compelling bit of information comes across my path, that I don't intend to do anything about it. As it stands right now, I'm putting this down to Apache. The only evidence I have that this wasn't Apache is that the tracks we followed were tracks made by shod horses. And the evidence I have that it was Apache is that two experienced stagecoach men – who work for Wells Fargo – saw these men with their own eyes and said they were Apache. So that's good enough for me."

"Do you have a lot of trouble with Apache?"

Tucker shrugged noncommittally, and Hughes could see that he was losing patience with the conversation.

"It comes and goes," Tucker said. "When they come off the reservation, yes, we have trouble with Apache around here. Back ten years ago, when Silver City was first being settled as a prospecting camp, the Apache killed a heap of people in various raids. These were their spiritual grounds a hundred years ago, or something. So they like to come up to the mountains and lift the hair off prospectors when they ain't on the reservation."

"And when they make raids like that, do they usually just do one and then run off to the Rio Grande?" Hughes said.

Tucker laughed.

"No, they don't. They usually hit as many camps as they can before the cavalry comes after them, then they disappear into the hills."

"Disappear?" Hughes said.

"Apache are hard to trail for very far," Tucker admitted. "Usually, we lose the trail in a hurry and then someone rides in to find the posse to report another camp has been raided. Then we ride after them toward that camp, pick up a trail until we lose it. That's usually how it happens. Sometimes we get lucky and wander up on the raiders, and then it's a shooting affair."

Hughes chewed his lip for a moment, thinking about other questions he had.

"Did you have a couple of Pinkerton men from the mine that rode with the posse?"

Tucker nodded.

"Yep, sure did. When we decided to turn back, they said they were going to keep trying to follow the trail."

"Think they'll have any luck?"

Tucker chuckled and rubbed his chin.

"If that cavalry scout can't track them Apache, I don't know why those Pinkerton boys would think they can."

"I hear that cavalry scout likes to drink," Hughes said.

Dangerous Dan Tucker laughed pretty hard at that.

"Look, Mr. Wells Fargo, I've known a fair share of

cavalry scouts. I've yet to meet one who stayed sober for any length of time. That don't mean he can't track."

Hughes left Dan Tucker to continue scowling at the folks coming and going on the street, and he went down the road to find the Express office.

The man seated at the desk behind the counter was a younger man, solidly built, and he wore a gun on his hip. He was not a typical Express office man.

"I'm Casper Bennett," the man said after Hughes introduced himself and told the man his business. "Roy Bennett was my daddy's cousin. I called him Uncle Roy, but they were cousins, not brothers."

"Hell, Casper, I'm sorry about what happened to him," Hughes said, not expecting to find the man's kin.

"Roy got me this job a year ago. He was a good man."

"I'm sure he was," Hughes said. "Wells Fargo doesn't hire slouches."

"There are a couple of things I'm trying to work through," Hughes said. "Any idea what happened to the livestock from the relay station?"

"I got them," Casper Bennett said. "Hired a couple of hands and went up there and got all the horses, a couple of milk cows and some pigs. They're at my place down below town."

"Were there any horses or ponies you didn't recognize?"

Casper shrugged.

"Honestly, I wouldn't have recognized all the

horses. Not the way Roy would have. Or Clint. They knew the horses. To me, it was just a corral full of horses."

"Okay," Hughes said. "How about unshod horses? Maybe horses or ponies that the Apache left in the corral?"

Casper shook his head.

"No, all the horses there were definitely Wells Fargo stagecoach stock."

"Were any horses missing? Did the Apache that attacked the station steal horses?"

Casper Bennett shook his head thoughtfully.

"No," he said slowly, doing a count in his mind. "No, if there were any missing horses, it wouldn't have been more than one or two. And if there were any extra horses, maybe one or two. I didn't know the horses, but I can say about how many they kept there. I certainly wouldn't report any stolen."

Hughes nodded thoughtfully. He did not want to say something that would spread rumors, so he left that alone for now.

"What about the books for the relay station?" Hughes said. "Any chance you have those, or have copies?"

Again, Casper shook his head.

"I don't have copies," he said. "I know for sure that Uncle Roy kept those in the safe."

"The missing safe," Hughes said.

"That's the one."

"Any idea who used that safe? I understand some of the prospectors around might have used it to keep valuables."

"Gibbons and White sent the payroll to that relay station directly every month," Casper said. "The payroll stayed in the safe until Cushman came to collect it."

"Anyone other than Cushman?"

"Uncle Roy would only have given it to Cushman. They knew each other pretty well, of course. But Cushman always rode with a guard. The only reason I know is because when I first come to Silver City, I stayed a couple of months out there at the relay station until Uncle Roy got me this job. So I saw him come out."

"Anyone else?" Hughes asked.

"No one else regular like that. A few other prospectors, maybe if they found a big gold nugget or had a heavy bag of dust that they were scared they would spend in a saloon, they might leave it with Uncle Roy for safekeeping. But nobody was coming out regular."

"Did Roy or Clint either one of them have any enemies?" Hughes asked.

Casper narrowed his eyes and gave Hughes a hard, appraising look.

"What are you getting at?" he said.

"I'm not getting at anything, Casper," Hughes said. "I'm just asking the questions I always ask."

"You don't think it was Apache?" Casper said.

"I think it was Apache," Hughes said. "Kays and Billy, from the stagecoach, they saw them. They wouldn't have any reason to lie."

He said it as a statement, but then left it hanging

there for Casper Bennett to grab hold to if he wanted.

"No," he said. "They wouldn't have any reason to lie."

"Then I have no reason to think it wasn't Apache," Hughes said.

"How well do you know Cushman?" Hughes asked.

"Not as well as Uncle Roy," Casper said. "But he comes to town quite a bit and does some business with me. He's all right."

Hughes frowned.

"All right is not a glowing recommendation," Hughes said.

"The man's a little anxious," Casper said. "He gets a lot of pressure from his company back in St. Louis, and he has to keep those miners happy. So he gets it coming and going. Every problem is a catastrophe, and about once a month I hear him say he's probably going to be fired."

"Is he honest?" Hughes asked.

Casper Bennett seemed to give it quite a bit of thought, but he finally nodded his head.

"He's honest."

- 7 -

Albert Fears had supper cooking on the campfire by the time Sequoia trotted into the campsite.

"Smells good," Hughes said. "I swear I smelled you cooking from a mile back."

As predicted, he'd arrived in camp after dark. Lucy Blake had set up a cot outside of her tent and was lying near the fire, looking up at the stars.

"Where'd you go after you left the fort?" she asked without looking at Hughes as he slid down out of his saddle.

"Rode into Silver City," Hughes said. He stretched

his legs a little. It had been some months since he'd ridden so much. The ride from Albuquerque had been relentless, and his inner thighs were so sore and stiff that he had to steady himself with a hand on Sequoia's back before he could start to walk the red roan to the corral.

"Did you learn anything interesting?"

"I'm not sure," Hughes said. "Possibly."

Lucy Blake rolled on her cot, planting an elbow and picking her head up to rest on her hand in a reclined position.

"Tell me," she said.

Hughes pursed waved some smoke out of his face and stepped away from it pulling Sequoia with him.

"Is it sporting if we share information now that we have turned this into a competition?" Hughes asked.

Lucy laughed.

"Perhaps not. If that's the way we'll do it, then we won't tell you what we learned at the fort."

Hughes sighed.

"That's fair enough," he said.

"It's interesting," Lucy teased at him.

"I'm sure it is," he said. "And likely it puts you closer to recovering the money than I am, so surely you don't want to give away valuable information."

Lucy now groaned in exasperation and sat up on the cot.

"What did you learn, Hughes?" she asked impatiently.

Hughes laughed.

"Let me turnout the horse, and then we can talk about it."

He led Sequoia into the barn where he removed the saddle and bags and blanket, and then took his time brushing her down. He brushed along her neck so that she craned and twisted her head, and Hughes chuckled at how much she enjoyed it. He was just about to untie her and put her in the corral with the rented horse and the Pinkertons' horses when a booming report rent the night air. Hughes dropped to a knee and had his Schofield in his fist in the space of a heartbeat.

Lucy shrieked immediately behind the gunfire, and Hughes at first thought she was hit, but he could see two figures over by the fire, and one was clearly Lucy charging into the darkness, getting away from the light of the fire that made her an easy target. The other was the unmistakable big frame of Albert Fears. For a moment Hughes wasn't sure what he was doing, but then he realized that Fears was moving the skillet off the fire so it wouldn't burn if there was about to be a shootout.

"Fears! Get out of there!" Hughes shouted at him, though as he scattered away from the red roan tied to the railing of a stall at the stable door, Hughes understood well that every man has his priorities.

More shots now interrupted the echo of the first. It was hard to be sure, but Hughes thought he could hear three distinct shooters. All of the shots seemed to be aimed at campfire. It took him a moment because he wasn't sure when the first shot was fired where it had come from, but the second burst of gunfire was clearly coming from the burned-out relay station off to Hughes' right. The camp was across the road, directly in front of him.

A second volley burst, and this time Hughes saw the muzzle flashes. The men shooting into the camp were at the far corner of the relay station, and indeed they were shooting into the campsite.

Albert Fears had collected a rifle, and he now sent a couple of shots back toward the relay station, but the men shooting at the camp immediately answered, each of them firing a shot, and then a second shot.

Hughes dashed to where he'd set his saddle and slid his Winchester rifle from its scabbard.

Sequoia danced around nervously. Hughes placed a hand on her hindquarter as he made his way behind her, thinking he could come out of the barn at the back and circle around behind the relay station.

As he came out the back door, a thunderous firefight broke loose – from the sound of it, Albert Fears and Lucy Blake were now both returning fire, and the three shooters were giving back all they received.

Rifle in hand, Hughes dashed from the back of the stables to the nearer back corner of the relay station. He didn't have a shot here. He would have to make his way along the length of the relay station, but he should easily manage to come in behind the men.

There was another great burst of gunfire, and before Hughes could move, he heard someone cry out in pain. It was a man's voice, so all he knew for sure was that it was not Lucy.

He stumbled over some debris that had been tossed out back after the fire and nearly fell headlong to the ground. The shooters on both sides had fallen silent. And then he heard the rhythmic thunder of horses galloping west, back toward Fort Bayard.

Hughes now made a dash to the far back corner of the burned-out station, but he could not see the men who'd opened fire on the campsite. He walked forward, his rifle up and ready to shoot, and he came out into the station yard without encountering anyone. And then Albert Fears appeared in the fire light, walking toward the road.

"Are you okay?" Hughes called to him.

"Not shot," Fears said. "But I think I dumped half our dinner into the fire."

"Miss Blake?" Hughes shouted into the darkness. And then Lucy came out from behind a large juniper bush, the firelight casting an orange glow on her.

"I'm fine," she said. "There were three of them, riding off to the west. I think I hit one of them."

"I couldn't make out if they were Apache or not," Albert Fears said.

"Oh, of course they were not," Lucy Blake said.

***

Hughes mounted on the spare horse he'd brought and rode out west a ways by himself, his Winchester draped over his saddle. He did not expect to find anything, and he was not disappointed.

In the weak light of the moon, the road showed up just a bit lighter shade of black than the ground covered with juniper and grass, but it would have been easy enough for those men to gallop some distance. Hughes had noted it as a good road, not a lot of holes or even bad ruts that might make a horse spill a rider, so they could have some confidence that they could move quickly in the low light.

He rode a mile, maybe a mile and a quarter, and when he saw nothing – and when no one took a shot at him – he turned back, believing the men were gone.

"All the same, we should take precautions tonight as if we expect them to come back," Hughes said.

They left the tents in place and the fire smoldering in its pit, but moved their bedrolls into the loft in the stable.

Albert Fears remained below in the shadows just inside the door of the stables to take the first watch of the night.

"The straw makes a better bed than the canvas cot," Lucy Blake observed, snuggling into her bedroll.

"We should think about taking rooms, either over at Fort Bayard or in Silver City," Hughes said. "We're too exposed here, and we've clearly angered someone."

"The Apache?" Lucy asked, with a sarcastic laugh.

"Maybe not," Hughes said. "When did you know we were not looking for Apache?"

"I always suspected," Lucy said. "Apache don't take safes."

"That was my first thought, too," Hughes said. "Not unless they have someone looking to sell them guns and ammunition."

"Well, I suppose that's true," Lucy said. "Except Apache don't usually ride saddled horses."

Hughes made a non-committal groan.

"Typically not," he said. "Raiders, they take what's available. It's not unheard of that an Apache might ride a saddled horse, but they'll ride a horse without saddle or blanket if they have to, and raiders almost always have to. They also don't shoe their horses, and when I was at Fort Bayard, I talked to one of the men from the posse. He said the horses they were trailing were all shod."

"You had better luck than I did at the fort. Lieutenant Stellman had little interest in talking to me." Then she added, sarcastically, "I think the lieutenant was intimidated by my eye patch."

Hughes chuckled.

"I talked to the corporal," Hughes said. "If one or two had saddles and shoed horses, I'd understand that. But all of them? It seems unlikely to me."

Lucy considered it for a moment in silence.

"Apache didn't come here and shoot at us, either," she said. "The Apache don't know we're here, and wouldn't care if they did."

"That's right," Hughes agreed.

"We've made someone nervous. Someone at the mine, or someone at the fort."

"Or someone in Silver City," Hughes said. "Remember, I rode there today."

"Who did you talk to?" Lucy asked.

"The deputy – Tucker – and the Wells Fargo Express agent in Silver City. Turns out his uncle was Roy Bennett."

"The manager here at this relay station?" Lucy said.

"The same."

"Is that of interest?" Lucy asked.

Hughes grunted.

"I don't know," he said. "He seemed like a decent sort to me. But if his uncle is operating the relay station, then it's likely that he has knowledge of what's inside the safe. Is two months' worth of payroll enough to tempt a man into killing his own uncle?"

"It is for some men," Lucy said reasonably.

"Yes. It is for some men."

Hughes changed the topic now.

"What about those other Pinkerton men?" he asked. "The guards at the mine?"

"The Pinkertons have private guards at mines all over the country," Lucy said. "Mines, steel plants, mills – anywhere there are large numbers of workers and the management is worried about strikes or trouble. But especially a mine like this, out here in Apache country. I did not know we had men here, but I guess I'm not surprised."

"Do you know where they are?" Hughes asked.

"I don't," Lucy said. "I was going to ask Lieutenant Stellman, but like I said, he had no interest in talking to me."

"Tucker said the Pinkertons decided to keep trying to follow the tracks. He said they followed the trail all the way down to the Rio Grande, but they lost them there."

"But a couple of Pinkerton payroll guards were going to keep at it?" Lucy said. "That's odd."

"I thought so, too."

Lucy took a deep breath.

"So we agree that there were never Apache renegades burning out the relay station?"

"We agree."

"And we agree that there was a ruse to steal a safe?"

"We agree."

"And it has to be someone who had knowledge that the payroll was at the relay station," Lucy said.

"Yep."

For a moment they were both silent in the darkness of the barn.

"Probably the two Pinkertons," Lucy said.

"Not acting alone," Hughes said. "But surely they were involved. And they got away by riding along with the posse."

Lucy groaned into the darkness.

"So what's next?" she asked.

"Not to tell you what to do, but I would suggest you go back to see Cushman," Hughes said. "If the Pinkertons orchestrated this, they probably had help from people at the mine. Those would be the people they associated with. Find out from Cushman who the Pinkertons associated with. Find out if anyone was missing from the mine the day of the robbery. It has to be that someone took the safe away from here and four men posed as Apache, waited for the stagecoach to show up, and then they rode off. At a minimum, there must have been six men involved, plus the Pinkertons if it was them."

"And Cushman might have been involved, too,"

Lucy said.

"Yes."

"So I should try to corroborate anything he says."

"That's just good detective work," Hughes agreed.

"What about you?" she asked.

"They did not go far with the safe," Hughes said. "I'm going to see if I can find it."

- 8 -

Cushman glanced several times from his tent at the woman with the eye patch and the big man with her. They were standing out by their buckboard, waiting to see him. He kept trying to look busy, though he knew they would not go away no matter how long he stalled.

"All right," he shouted to them. "You can have five minutes."

Cushman sat on a chair beside a table inside his canvas tent. On the table in front of him was a camp desk. It was a tall, rectangular box. The front of it folded down to become a writing platform, while the box contained a number of slots and drawers for everything from papers to his ink jar, candles, wax and other necessities. The camp desk was his prized possession. He'd been a young man in the war, toting messages for officers, and he'd seen a hundred camp desks in the tents of majors and colonels and generals. The camp desk came to symbolize for the young man power and prestige. Only an important man had a camp desk. Meticulously, Cushman kept it oiled and clean. When visitors came to his tent, whether the men at the mines or someone from outside, Cushman liked to bring them into his tent where he would sit beside the desk so that people could see it, see him with it.

To underscore his point, Cushman removed his watch chain and set his watch down on the camp desk.

"Five minutes," he repeated. "I'm very busy, and I'm only giving you five minutes because Gibbons and White hired the Pinkertons and I feel duty-bound to cooperate with you."

Lucy Blake smiled prettily at him. Despite the scar on her cheek, and even the eye patch, she remained a stunningly attractive woman. The eye patch gave her an aura of severity that was not without its benefits in her line of work, but it was a pretty severity.

"Mr. Cushman," Lucy said, adopting a kill-him-with-kindness attitude, "I understand that you are very busy, and especially so now, and I appreciate you taking the time to talk to us. This is my associate Mr. Fears, I'm not certain that you met yesterday."

"I saw him out by the wagon," Cushman said, and he gave Albert Fears a civil nod.

"We had an incident at our camp last evening," Lucy

said.

"An incident?" Cushman said.

"I'm afraid so," Lucy said. "After dark, several men took some shots at us in our camp."

"Shots!" Cushman exclaimed. "You mean they shot at you?"

Lucy remained calm.

"Yes, Mr. Cushman. Someone shot at us."

"Apache?" he asked.

"Well, it was after dark, so we do not know who it was. My associate, Mr. Hughes, gave chase, but he could not catch up to the men. We returned fire, and I do think it's possible I struck one of the men."

Cushman seemed genuinely alarmed at the turn of events.

"Shot at a woman?" he said. "And you think it was the same Apache who burnt the relay station?"

Lucy shrugged her shoulders a little without saying anything one way or another.

"It was very frightening, I can tell you that. In the dark of the night, Mr. Fears was preparing our supper, and the stillness of evening was rent by the sharp report of gunfire. Very frightening."

"I'm sure it was," Cushman said.

"But that is not why I am here," Lucy said.

"It's not?" Cushman said.

"No. I was talking after the incident with my associate, Mr. Hughes, and we both wondered if anyone from the mine was missing on the day the relay station was burned."

"Missing?" Cushman asked.

"Yes. Away from the mining operation. What we were wondering is if you keep any record of men who are off the job for any reason. We thought perhaps if someone had gone to town for supplies or to deliver mail or anything of the sort, maybe they saw something that could be helpful to us."

Cushman rubbed his chin thoughtfully. He turned to his camp desk and began sliding out ledgers from one slot in the cabinet.

"I keep a log of sick and absent," he said. He found the right ledger and pulled it out from the slot. He riffled through the pages until he came to the correct date.

"Willy Slack busted his toe with a sledge hammer. He was laid up that day. Laid up for the two days before and three days after, too. And Josh Robinson and Daniel McCay rode over to Fort Bayard in a buckboard to pick up supplies. The cook, Johnny Washington, he rode with Robinson and McCay."

"What about the Pinkerton men?" Lucy said. "Were they around?"

Cushman thought about it for a moment, squinting one eye as he tried to recollect.

"Sure, they were here," he said. "I don't keep track of their comings and goings in the ledger, but they're almost always here, anyway. And I know they were here that day, because they rode up to the relay station when the stagecoach man rode over here to the mine to tell us what happened."

"Are you aware that the posse has returned?" Lucy asked.

"Someone said so," Cushman said.

"But the Pinkerton men have not returned."

"No. I reckon they kept on with the pursuit – as well they should. That payroll is as much their responsibility as it is mine."

Lucy was making notes in a notebook as Cushman talked, and she looked over the names again.

"Was Mr. Slack in the camp?" she asked.

"Hell yes, he was," Cushman said. "Willy couldn't walk after smashing his toe. He's still limping all around the place."

"Are those the only missing men?" Lucy asked.

"None of them were missing," Cushman said, suddenly getting a little aggravated. "What are you driving at, Miss Blake?"

"I'm not driving at anything, Mr. Cushman. I'm just trying to find anyone who might have seen something or might know something that could be helpful to us. Robinson, McCay, and Washington – would it be possible for me to talk to them?"

Cushman shrugged.

"They're down in the mines now. Well, Robinson and McCay are. Washington, he's going to be at our mess hall, I reckon."

"Then we'll go and have a word with Mr. Washington while you send someone to fetch Robinson and McCay for us," Lucy said.

Cushman said, "Wait. Robinson and McCay are working."

"I'm sure it won't take too long to fetch them from the mine," Lucy said. "We'll be glad to wait."

Lucy and Albert Fears were already standing up. Cushman wasn't exactly sure that he'd agreed to let Lucy talk to Washington, and he was certain he hadn't agreed to fetch Robinson and McCay. But already the Pinkertons were moving out of his tent.

"Which way is the mess hall?" Lucy asked.

Cushman pointed them in the right direction to the mess hall and then sent someone into the mines to get Robinson and McCay.

They found a man at a fire behind the mess hall working over a large pot. The mining operation was mostly a cluster of white canvas tents, but there were a few stick-built structures, the mess hall being one of them. The mess hall wasn't much to look at, just a long, narrow building made from plank boards. Several windows on both of the long sides meant that it was full of flies and weather, but it at least gave the men a dry place to eat in rain storms and a shady place to eat in the heat of summer. The mess hall had two long rows of tables pushed up against each other, and Lucy figured about half the men from the mining camp could fit in there at any one time. There was no kitchen, just a large storeroom at one end and the long dining hall. The cooking was done on a large fire pit behind the mess hall.

"The key to tasty beans is you cook the bacon in the pot first, slice it up good and let all that grease from the bacon flavor the beans," he said. He'd watched Lucy Blake and Albert Fears approaching him, and when they were within earshot, he gave them his advice for cooking beans.

"It smells good," Lucy said politely. "Is that the standard fare here?"

"Beans and bacon," Washington said. "Standard fare. Sometimes, if one of the boys shoots a pronghorn or a whitetail, we'll have stew with onion and potatoes. But beans and bacon is what the company pays for."

"My name is Lucy Blake. I am a detective with the Pinkerton Agency."

Washington, a grizzled man who was probably much younger than he appeared, wrinkled his brow.

"A woman detective?" he asked.

"That's right. Are you Washington?"

"They call me Cookie, but Washington is my surname."

"Mr. Washington, I understand you were outside of the camp the day the relay station was attacked."

"Damned Apache," Washington said. "I knew Roy Bennett. He was a good man, and I sure was sorry he got killed."

"Do you remember that day, being out of camp?" Lucy asked.

Washington sat on a camp chair beside the fire, stirring the contents of his pot.

"Sure, I remember. Rode over to the store at Fort Bayard to get supplies. Four sacks of flour. Two sacks of sugar. A barrel of molasses. Enough bacon to last us a month."

"Did you see any sign of the Apache the attacked the stagecoach station?" Lucy asked.

Washington furrowed his brow.

"Well, we wouldn't have," he said. "We rode to Fort Bayard, and that's the other direction from the relay station. And I don't reckon even the Apache would go that close to the fort."

"No," Lucy said. "I don't reckon. We're trying to track down anyone who might have witnessed anything. Did you see anyone else out that day? Did you pass by anyone at all?"

Washington scratched at his whiskered chin.

"I saw some folks about at Fort Bayard, of course, but I don't reckon I passed anyone on the road. It was just a quiet ride to the store and back."

"When you got back, had the relay station already been attacked?"

"You know what," Washington said. "When I was coming back, I saw the smoke off in the east. I remember wondering what it was that was on fire. And then I got back to the camp and started to unload the supplies, and it wasn't long after that someone rode into the camp and said there'd been an attack at the relay station."

The man's story seemed likely enough, and he told it in a straight-forward way. Nothing about Washington or his story aroused any suspicion.

"It makes a man nervous, knowing you've got Apache roaming around these hills," Washington said.

"They're not likely to attack the mining camp, are they?" Lucy said.

"No, but that very day that I'm out there driving to Fort Bayard, there's Apache killing white folks just a few

PRINCIPLES OF DIETING AND EATING

*D*on't blame yourself if you have been seduced into dieting trends in the past. Friends, we live in a world where thin women and masculine men are thought to be the healthiest. As a result, having a thin body has become the accepted symbol of self-confidence, wellbeing, and accomplishment. If you don't fit in that category, you might find yourself unnecessarily feeling unhealthy, lazy, or inferior.

The dieting industry has taken advantage of this warped philosophy by making people believe that they have to be thin to feel worthy. When you feel worse about your body, there is no doubt that you will eventually succumb to societal pressure and spend your money on different diets on a quest to attain the "perfect body."

Have you ever asked yourself why dieting is a billion-dollar industry? Well, allow me to break it down for you; it is because diets don't work! You see, when one diet fails, you have hundreds of other options to select from. Let's not risk getting ahead of ourselves yet. This chapter will let you in on the principles of dieting and eating. You will discover why the diets that cost a fortune don't work, and I will also help you understand the different types of restrictive or unsustainable fad diets. Later in the chapter, we will cover more on eating disorders and weight stigma.

After that, you will be ready to learn about the factors that affect your food choices, including how you can control your sugar cravings. Toward the end of this chapter, we'll talk about the golden rules of eating and how you can rewire your brain to align with your goal and your healthy lifestyle choices.

WHY DIETS DON'T WORK

Several studies have shown that dieting could produce impressive results in the initial stages, but 95% of the subjects regain weight in one to five years after stopping. Moreover, the studies also revealed that many diets lead to weight loss and lower blood pressure, but the results quickly disappear after only one year.

miles from here. What if they'd come across me out on the road?"

"There were only four of them," Lucy said reasonably.

"That may be, but I'm only one of me."

Lucy glanced at her notebook.

"And McCay and Robinson," she said.

"McCay and Robinson?" Washington said. "What about 'em?"

Lucy shrugged.

"Between the three of you, I wouldn't expect the Apache to try to attack you on the road."

Washington frowned at her for a moment, clearly puzzled.

"Except there wasn't three of us," he said. "It was just me."

Lucy narrowed her eyes at him.

"Robinson and McCay did not ride with you to Fort Bayard?"

Washington shook his head.

"No, ma'am. Nobody rode with me. Nobody hardly ever does."

Lucy looked at Albert Fears and Fears shrugged his shoulders.

"But Mr. Cushman said that Johnny Robinson and Daniel McCay rode with you to Fort Bayard," Lucy said.

Even as she said it, the three of them heard the

sound of horses riding hard out of camp. Lucy hurried around the side of the mess hall and saw two men riding away from the mine's stable, their horses at a thundering gallop up a winding path that led from the camp up to the main road.

"Mr. Fears," Lucy said. "Hurry along to Mr. Cushman and see if you can ascertain the identity of those two riders."

Fears set off at shuffling jog, the quickest step he ever mustered, and Lucy returned to Washington.

"Thank you for your time, Mr. Washington," she said, and she made a quick note in her notebook that Washington said he was alone on his supply run to Fort Bayard.

She was halfway to Cushman's tent when Albert Fears and Cushman met her.

"I don't know what's got into those two boys," Cushman said. "But that was Robinson and McCay. I swear I told them to meet you over by the mess hall, but they just rode right on out of camp. I don't know what they were thinking or where they're bound for."

***

Calvin Hughes spent the morning in what seemed likely to prove a fruitless search. He was looking for wagon tracks on a stagecoach road full of tracks. None of the tracks were deep ruts. The road here was compacted, not the crusty caliche of the lower desert, but loose gravel and hard packed sand. Had it been one or two wagons through here over the past month, he'd have easily found the tracks he was looking for. The rainy season was well over, and there'd been no significant rainfall to disturb the evidence on the ground.

But there were not one or two tracks along the road.

Prospectors leading mule teams or driving wagons came across this road. The soldiers from Fort Bayard used this road. The stagecoaches from Silver City to Mesilla and Albuquerque came this way every couple of days. Freighters bringing in supplies to Silver City.

The more the Wells Fargo man dropped to a knee and tried to follow what appeared to him to be the freshest tracks, the more he realized that everything ran together.

He limited his search to those tracks left around the burned-out relay station.

Whoever took the safe must have pulled their wagon into the yard of the relay station. But there were countless signs of wagon wheels in the yard of the station, all mixed in with the more distinct track of the stagecoaches, that all mixed in with each other.

Hughes sighed heavily as his eyes began to lose focus looking at lines in the dirt.

The shadows receded, crawling back into themselves as the sun lifted in the sky. The air in the high hills was fresh and clean, and there was something, some weed or tree, that gave off a fragrant scent and Hughes caught a whiff of it from time to time as he walked around the burned-out relay station.

Another idea struck him, and he went to the corral where he caught the red roan with a lead rope and brought her into the cover of the stables. He brushed her off and saddled her, and then walked with the horse down the road to the east, away from the mine, away from Fort Bayard, and away from Silver City.

As he led the red roan along the road, he shared with the horse his thinking. Hughes was no different from a drifter or a drover – men who spent long hours in the saddle often found their closest confidante was their horse, and when they shared their thinking, their horse was not only agreeable but also sympathetic. A man could talk for hours to his mount, and the only responses would be those he yearned to hear.

"They'd not have risked taking the safe down the stagecoach road," Hughes said. "And they'd not have risked going west with it for fear of encountering someone on the ride back toward the mine and the fort. So once they got that safe loaded, they'd have wanted to hurry to get it off the road."

Hughes watched the tracks as he led the red roan along the road to the east. Still all the tracks mingled in with each other, and there was nothing worthwhile to see.

"Somewhere they had to find a road or a trail that took them off this road. They waited for the stagecoach and let the stagecoach see them, and what the stagecoach men saw was Apache. They left tracks for the posse to follow, because those four men, whether they were truly Apache or just men posing as Apache, were nothing more than bait to lure the posse away from the true intent – stealing the safe.

They walked up a hill. The grade was not steep, necessarily, but the hill was long, and Hughes found himself growing winded as they reached the top.

Below him, the road fell away into another valley, and then traced up and around another tall hill opposite. It went on like this for many miles until the land began to level out toward the Rio Grande. But standing atop the precipice, Hughes had a good view of the surrounding hillsides, sandy brown but dotted with green juniper and pinyon.

He almost gave up, satisfied that he was working off a premise that wouldn't hold true, but he at last decided to mount up and ride Sequoia at least to the opposite hilltop. If he found nothing by then, he would turn around and ride back to the campsite.

Every gap between the juniper looked like a path, though Hughes knew each one would prove to be a maze, winding through the big evergreen bushes and leading to nowhere. But when he was about thirty yards below the top of the hill, he spotted up ahead a wider gap between two juniper. The horse felt the flash of excitement that went through Hughes, and she quickened her step toward the spot.

"You could fit a wagon through there," Hughes said, and as he looked at the gap between the bushes, he realized that there was an unmistakable trail leading north.

Now he slid out of the saddle and squatted down on one knee, and there he found the faint impression of wagon wheels – undeniable evidence that indeed someone had taken a wagon up this way. And he saw hoof prints, suggesting riders had come this way, also.

He couldn't guess how long it had been since those tracks were made. Fresh tracks were easier. If someone had ridden through here in the last day or two, he'd be able to say for sure. These were more faded, but they were undisturbed. Though the path was clearly one that had seen plenty of use, Hughes thought it must have been some times since people regularly traveled this way.

"We might have something," he said, stepping back

into the saddle.

Having been shot at once already, Hughes decided to ride on with his Winchester across his lap, and he drew it from its scabbard and gave the horse leg to get moving down the trail.

He proceeded with caution and at an easy pace. The juniper bushes grew seven or eight feet high, and were just as wide, and it would be nothing for a man laying in ambush to hide behind one. In fact, a man on a horse could hide behind one. But as he continued along the path, there was no disputing this was a cut trail leading to somewhere, even as it wound around some big bushes. Whole bushes had been cut out and rolled off the trail like tumbleweeds. The growth of branches had been stunted by wagons coming through and tearing them. At some point, maybe a year or two or five previous, this was a path that had seen a good deal of traffic, and not Indian traffic, either. This was a prospector's road.

As morning wore into afternoon, the trail seemed to settle into a pattern of its own, following the natural contour of the land, cutting like a ridge above a dry wash and following a natural valley. And then the trail cut hard to the left and began to switch back and forth, rising higher up a steep slope. As he climbed, taller pines interspersed among the squat juniper, and the places between the juniper bushes began to fill in with scrub oak, now bare of leaves and looking harsh and gray, and Hughes realized there was a new chill in the air. The trail bent over a ridge, and it was almost as if Hughes was transported to a different world. Ponderosa pine stretched high above him now, and the juniper were all gone. In truth, the transition had been gradual as he climbed higher, but he was starkly aware of it now as the landscape shifted with the higher

How you will feel after making a certain decision or behavior is important. Experts warn that your thoughts, emotions, and behaviors are all connected. Therefore, how you feel after making that decision could result in either positive or negative thoughts, which will inform your next behavior. If you are going to feel bad after going off your food plan, don't make that decision. You can find a way of remaining social, for instance, just popping in and leaving early.

- **How often do you go out?** If you have been going out a lot lately, you might want to rethink your goals and decide what carries more weight. You ought to find a balance in your life. A healthy lifestyle means you are okay with the balance.

- **Consider what you are going to eat or drink.** Is it worth it? If you feel it is not worth it, then don't do it. Never feel like you need to succumb to peer pressure. You can make plans to meet your friends later and suggest places you feel comfortable meeting them, which offers options for everyone.

HOW TO STAY ON TRACK

The best solution is to go for social events but find ways of staying on track. Although this could probably be easier said than done, there are smart strategies you can use to keep you in charge of the situation. They include:

- **Be flexible in your thinking.** You need to be creative to ensure that your social plans are effective. For example, if you usually go to the gym after work and have a happy hour, you can wake up earlier and work out in the morning. This ensures that you stick to your plan and be social without feeling guilty.

- **Check out the menu before time.** If you are going to a restaurant or bar, this is critical. This helps you decide precisely what you will order; hence, spend more time socializing than on what you will eat.

- **Offer to bring something.** If you have been invited to a party, offer to bring a dish. This opens the door for you to bring what you will enjoy eating and is part of your plan.

- **Inform your hosts that you will need to leave early.** If you have an early run in the altitude.

Traveling through the pine forest, Hughes crossed one ridge, and then another. He dropped down into a canyon and realized that the sun was beginning to dip. He checked his watch and discovered his morning exploration had turned into a day-long affair. He did not know if he would even make it back to the camp at the relay station by dark.

But he pressed on forward, convinced that this trail was taking him someplace important.

Tracing his route in his mind, Hughes imagined he was now somewhere north of Fort Bayard. Possibly he'd cut far enough west that he was north of Silver City.

And then ahead he heard a noise, strange to his ears at first because he'd heard nothing for hours apart from Sequoia's hooves on the rocky path, the birds and a gentle breeze in the trees. And then he realized he was hearing a creek running somewhere ahead of him.

The trail cut harder to the north, and the valley slipped away to his left now, and he craned his neck and saw the creek running down below him. The trail dipped lower toward the creek, and after riding about a hundred yards he came close to the floor of the valley, and near the creek, and there ahead in a clearing he saw a half dozen small buildings.

Hughes slid from his saddle and walked Sequoia off the trail a piece and knotted her reins on a pine branch.

Now he moved slowly toward the buildings, taking his time and walking from tree to tree so that he would not be seen. He heard no voice, saw no movement. The buildings were made of cut logs, obviously timber from the area. Broken casks and furniture littered the area, rusty old pans and even a few rusty tools were scattered about.

Hughes quickly became convinced the place was abandoned, and he walked up to one of the old cabins and found evidence that wild animals had been the most recent evidence.

But in the yard between the buildings that led down to the creek, Hughes saw what he came to find.

Satisfied that the place was abandoned and there was no one here, Hughes walked back along the road to fetch his horse. When he returned, he went to the safe.

The big safe was laying on its back. It had wheels on the base, which probably made the job easier for the men who stole it. The door was busted open, probably with the use of a chisel and sledge hammer, but the tools used to open it were gone.

Beside it on the ground were a few papers and letters, a couple of ledger books, but the safe itself was empty.

Hughes picked up one of the ledgers and flipped through the pages. It recorded deposits made by Gibbons and White and withdrawals made by Cushman. They were all marked "payroll." Roy Bennett had been thorough in his accounting and he'd left detailed descriptions. Other deposits included things like the weight of a bag of gold dust or a gold nugget and the name of the person who stored it. Most of them were trivial amounts, though surely important to the person who deposited the piece with the Wells Fargo man at the relay station.

In another ledger, Bennett noted letters received and held for men who Hughes believed were probably prospectors in the area. This ledger also noted that two horses in the station's corral were being held for a local man, and a buckboard in the stables was there for yet another man.

He looked through the other papers. There were not many of them and they included legal documents, probably being held on behalf of people who had no other place to keep an important document. Hughes found a copy of a claim made on Bear Creek and a copy of a timber lease and a roughly-written document establishing a partnership for a store over near Fort Bayard.

"I reckon these are all documents being held by Wells, Fargo & Company," Hughes said to the horse. "So we should tote them back."

He put the documents into the horse's saddlebags, and he left Sequoia to roam at-will while he picked through the camp.

Down at the creek he found where the men who'd been here had set up a small diversion dam and dug a millrace and had some sluice boxes set up. A broken cradle and some rusty pans, one that had been used for target practice, suggested the claim here had panned out and the outfit had just walked out on it.

Maybe that was a couple of years ago.

Hughes figured those men were long gone, and had nothing to do with the theft, murder, and arson back at the relay station.

- 9 -

The light touched Lucy Blake's face, warm and bright, and she woke with a start to the smell of fresh straw and an empty hay loft.

Down below she could hear Albert Fears snoring.

She eased herself up off the bed of straw, leaving her blanket where it was, and walked softly over to the edge of the loft where she could see the big man below her. Albert Fears had said he'd keep watch, but he was sitting in a chair and leaning against a stall door, asleep and snoring at such a volume that Lucy assumed he'd been asleep for some time.

Lucy wrinkled her nose against some odor, and then realized it was she herself who needed a bath. They'd been days on the road in the hot sun, and now she was two nights sleeping in a hay loft.

But the smell was of less concern to her than the absence of the Wells Fargo man.

After watching Robinson and McCay ride away from the mine, Lucy and Albert Fears returned to the camp at the burned-out relay station. She was eager to share this latest development with Hughes, but he wasn't around. The sun dipped low over the mountains to the west, and Hughes still did not turn up. Albert Fears cooked dinner enough for three of them, and while he did, Lucy sat with a Winchester rifle at the back of the burned-out Wells Fargo relay station. Still, Hughes did not turn up. Lucy climbed into the hayloft to sleep, and Albert Fears took up a position in the stable, and still there was no word from Hughes.

Lucy dropped her high-heeled boots over the side of the loft, and the double thumps roused Fears who came up with the rifle in hand.

"It's just me," Lucy said, climbing down the ladder from the hayloft.

All the same, Fears walked to the open doors of the stable and looked around.

"Hughes never turned up," Fears said.

"No, I don't suppose he did."

"Should we worry?" Fears asked.

"Probably not. Mr. Hughes is his own man, and certainly capable of taking care of himself."

Fears leaned the rifle against the door of the stable and stretched, raising his great arms up into the air so that his shirt pulled loose from the top of his pants and exposed his stomach. He was not a particularly pleasant companion, Lucy decided, but he did seem devoted to her.

"So what's on for today?" he asked.

"I think we should return to the mine and see if we can find those two men who rode out on us yesterday," Lucy said. "Those men did not flee an interview with us because they have nothing to hide."

Fears laughed.

"I reckon that's true enough," he said. "So, you and Mr. Hughes don't think this was Apache at all?"

"Not at all, Mr. Fears," Lucy said. "It seems obvious to me now that whoever did this came to the relay station and killed the two men here – Bennett and Thacker. Some among their number took the safe, I assume by a wagon, and left out of here. And four men, dressed as Apache, set fire to the relay station. Then they waited for the stagecoach. As soon as they knew the men on the stagecoach had seen them, they dashed out of here."

"They let the stagecoach men see them?"

"Yes. So that everyone would believe they were Apache."

Fears nodded. He knew he was slow to catch on, but he appreciated that Miss Blake never made him feel dumb about it.

"You think it was those men from the copper mine?"

Lucy shrugged and raised her eyebrows, both of

them, which made her eye patch move in a way that made Albert Fears uncomfortable.

"It's certainly possible, Mr. Fears. They told Cushman they were going with the cook to get supplies at Fort Bayard, but the cook told us that Robinson and McCay did not go with him. And, riding away from the mine yesterday was certainly suspicious behavior. Wouldn't you say?"

Fears nodded.

"Yes, ma'am. Very suspicious."

"But they did not act alone, if they were involved. We also have two missing Pinkerton men," Lucy said.

"I've worked with a lot of Pinkerton detectives," Albert Fears said. "In fact, I used to guard the payroll for a place real similar to the Santa Rita mine. That was over in Arizona Territory. But I'd be real surprised if a Pinkerton would have done something like this. They swore an oath, Miss Blake."

Lucy smiled sympathetically at Albert Fears.

"Oh, Mr. Fears, no man is incorruptible. In our line of work, everyone must be a suspect until he is proved not to be a suspect."

Fears shrugged.

"I reckon so," he said. "But I still don't see a Pinkerton stealing a payroll he's promised to guard."

Albert Fears made breakfast, and after they ate, he and Lucy Blake broke down one of the two tents.

"We'll find a hotel, either at Fort Bayard or in Silver City if we must. But I don't fancy spending another night here."

"I didn't start to doze off until morning time," Fears said defensively.

"It's not only that," Lucy said. "But I need a bath and a decent bed, and you need a night's sleep that is untainted from having to keep watch."

Although, in truth, Lucy was equally concerned with what time Albert Fears dozed off and what might have transpired while he was asleep. So they broke down the tent and packed their belongings onto the wagon.

Still, Calvin Hughes did not turn up.

Lucy left a note for the Wells Fargo man, letting him know that he could find them at Fort Bayard, or possibly Silver City, that they were going to find a hotel. She left the note sitting on top of his trunk inside his tent.

"On the way, we will stop at the Santa Rita mine."

**

If he was stiff and sore before, Calvin Hughes felt much worse now. He'd used his saddle blanket for a bed and his saddle for a pillow. He covered himself with his canvas duster he wore to protect his good coat, but it did almost nothing to keep him comfortable through the chill of the night.

Hughes and Sequoia made it out of the pine forest before nightfall, but darkness caught them still many miles from the camp. So he bedded down where a juniper bush gave him some protection from the night breeze and made a supper out of cold jerky and crackers. At some point during the night, Sequoia became restless. Hughes had looped mare's lead rope under him as he slept so that if the horse alerted to something it would wake him. When she started to shift nervously, Hughes woke up and stayed awake for some time. He heard nothing in the open land and decided the horse had likely spooked at nothing or, if there was something, maybe coyotes some distance away. Regardless, his sleep was disturbed, and he found it difficult to go back to sleep.

When morning broke, Hughes saddled the red roan and started back on the trail, working his way south and east, back toward the relay station and the camp where he expected to find Lucy Blake and Albert Fears.

The ledgers and the broken safe proved nothing. If Apache had stolen the safe, they would have taken it somewhere and broken into it the same as anyone else would have. But clearly whoever stole the safe did not leave the relay station with the men who rode east to the Rio Grande. The evidence, scant as it was, so far bore out the theory that whoever murdered the men, stole the safe, and burned the relay station wanted to leave the impression that they were Apache.

Hughes had found the wagon that had been used to transport the safe. It had been pushed down into a ravine not far from the abandoned mining camp where he'd found the safe. Maybe the men who murdered the two men and burned out the relay station also stole the wagon from the relay station. The ledger book indicated that someone had stored a wagon at the relay station, but Hughes did not remember seeing one in the stable. Anyone would expect the relay station to have a buggy, at least, and probably a buckboard. But it seemed to Hughes that the thieves had been lucky that the wagon was there. If it hadn't been there, they never would have been able to get the safe away from the relay station.

The Wells Fargo man twisted himself in the saddle and stretched one arm up into the air, then the other. Whatever rock he slept on just below his right shoulder blade felt as if it was still embedded in his back. That knot would not work itself out with a few stretches, and Hughes frowned as he conceded that it would be with him all day.

The morning light touched the land all around him now, gentle in a way that made the land glow easy beneath the shade of the juniper. In an hour or two, everything would be hard and bright, and the chill of morning would burn away under the glare of the sun.

Sequoia seemed to understand that their job along this trail had come to an end, and she worked herself into a pretty good pace, quickly covering the distance with a comfortable lope. Hughes prized the horse for her comfortable gait, and now she proved her worth.

They slipped down out of the high hills and followed the trail as it snaked along beside a dry wash down in a valley, and then wound up over a big hill, and an hour later, Hughes found himself back on the stagecoach road. A couple of hours after noon, horse and rider came within sight of the lone tent sitting outside the burned-out relay station.

"Looks like we've been abandoned," Hughes said.

He unsaddled the horse and brushed her down and turned her out in the corral to rest. If he went anywhere else today, he would take the spare mount he'd brought along to give Sequoia a break. She'd covered a lot of distance in the last two days.

The Wells Fargo agent found the letter from Lucy

Blake inside his tent, and he found it frustratingly vague. She told him nothing of her investigation the previous day and said only that she and Albert Fears had decided to get rooms at a hotel, but she did not even direct him to a specific town where they might be found. Had they gone to Fort Bayard or on in to Silver City?

Hughes left his tent standing, but he brought his cot and trunk out of the tent and into the stable. Albert Fears had left him provisions enough to make a dinner out of beans and bacon, and he now prepared himself something to eat.

After he'd eaten, Hughes found a table and chair in the stable, and he sat for a long while going through the ledgers he'd found near the safe.

As a Wells Fargo agent, sometimes his job involved going through the books at express offices, looking for irregularities that might lead him to missing money. He took no pleasure from those times when he had to arrest an express office manager who was skimming off the top, but Hughes had become adept at scanning the ledgers and finding entries that made no sense.

He did not know what he was looking for now.

Roy Bennett kept these books – his initials were on every entry. And Roy Bennett was murdered and his safe stolen. Hughes had no suspicion that Bennett had stolen money, and so he had no suspicion that he would find an irregularity in the ledgers. Instead, the ledgers were like a glimpse into the daily life at the relay station. Hughes had dates for when Bennett or Thacker went to town for supplies. He had entries for the people who did business with the relay station. Prospectors in the area used the relay station like a combination of bank and store and livery.

They bought supplies from Bennett, they kept their valuables in his safe, they sometimes kept horses and mules in his corral.

As he went through the two ledgers, Hughes came to realize that some of the transactions represented a kind of side business for Bennett. Storing a wagon, selling hay or nails or a can of beans – these were all things Bennett did for his own benefit. He marked up the price of the beans and nails and lanterns and candles that he sold, and he made a little profit for himself. When a prospector left his horse or mule at the relay station's corral for a few days, Bennett profited.

Hughes could not see where Bennett did anything wrong. The merchandise he sold appeared to have been bought originally with his own money. Bennett's records were meticulous, separating his side business from Wells Fargo business. The man's sense of personal ethics shone in the ledgers. If anything, Bennett might have been feeding stock with hay bought by Wells Fargo for the stagecoach stock, but Hughes could hardly fault the man for that. It appeared that whoever killed Roy Bennett took the life of a straight, stand-up man, and that made Hughes all that much angrier at the murders committed here. Thacker was likely just as decent and honest as Roy Bennett.

The banking was all Wells Fargo business. Bennett made no profit from the Gibbons and White payroll. The cash came in on a Wells Fargo stagecoach and Bennett put it in a Wells Fargo safe until Cushman came along to collect it. No additional money changed hands. When he kept gold dust or other valuables for are prospectors, he appeared to do it simply as a favor to the local men who had no nearby bank. Nobody – neither Wells Fargo nor Roy Bennett – profited from a prospector who left a bag of placer gold in the relay station's safe.

As he went through the ledger entries, Hughes easily imagined life at the relay station. Hard work when the stagecoaches came in. Pleasant distractions when local prospectors came to do business. Lonely hours spent between Bennett and Thacker, likely filled with friendly card games and lengthy discussions about upcoming meals.

The stream of sunlight coming through the stable door shortened as Hughes read the ledger entries, and the shadows inside the stable grew darker until at last he began having trouble reading the pencil markings.

Hughes closed the ledgers and put them on a shelf where they'd kept horse tack.

He stretched his back and started to walk out into the last of the sunlight when he heard coming from the east a couple of riders.

Quickly, Hughes slid his Schofield six-shooter from its holster, opened the top-break gun and checked that all six chambers were loaded. He returned the gun to the holster but left the leather thong down off the hammer. Then he stepped toward the stable door, but he stayed back in the shadows. He wanted to see who was coming along the road before they saw him.

Two men, both wearing long dusters over dark suits. They both wore dark hats. They might have been twins they were so identical to each other, and if he'd been in a dark suit with a duster, Albert Fears might have made the twins triplets. Both men wore a thick layer of dust on their clothes and hats, their faces were crusty, and they appeared weary of their saddles.

As he watched them from the shadows, the men

were speaking to each other in low tones. They were looking directly at Hughes' tent, and now turning their horses toward it.

"Howdy," Hughes said, stepping from the shadows of the stable and out into the waning sunlight.

Both men started. And both men went for their guns.

"No need to pull iron," Hughes said, showing the men his hands and giving a friendly smile. "My name is Hughes. I'm with Wells Fargo."

The two men exchanged a glance and one of them spoke.

"I'm Pickens and this is Woods," he said, but he left off any other specifics.

"You boys wouldn't happen to be Pinkertons?" Hughes said.

"How'd you know that?" Woods asked.

"I've talked to Cushman down at the mine, and I talked to the posse when they rode back. I knew you boys had continued the pursuit of the Apache."

"That's right," Pickens said.

"I'm guessing you weren't successful?" Hughes said, making the statement a question to invite an answer.

"You're guessing right," Pickens said. "Never did track them farther than the Rio Grande. What are you doing here?"

"Wells Fargo relay station," Hughes said with a toss of the head toward the burned-out station. "Somebody's got to deal with this."

The two men glanced at each other again, and Woods shrugged.

"We're trying to make the mine before sundown," he said.

"Cutting it close," Hughes said.

"Right. So we're going to ride on. You take care. There's Apache loose somewhere."

Hughes touched the tip of his hat as the two men started their horses back along the road. He watched them as they went on up the road. The horses moved slow. They looked weary, and covered in a gray dust – the gray dust of the caliche of the desert down near the Rio Grande.

Hughes chewed his lip for a moment, even after the men topped the hill and disappeared from sight. He had no proof of anything, but those Pinkerton guards had the look of men who'd ridden with determination to catch their suspects.

Calvin Hughes shook his head. He took a walk around the burned-out ruins of the relay station. If there was a clue in there, it was all ash now. The fire had been thorough. He walked over to the stables and looked around back.

He found a buckboard wagon, but it was painted with the Wells Fargo lettering, faded and chipped though it was, on the back gate. This was the wagon that Bennett and Thacker used to make supply runs to town. Hughes remembered the wagon that was mentioned in the ledger. That was surely the one he'd seen in the ravine at the mining camp in the mountains. In addition to the valuables stolen from the safe, someone had lost a good, solid wagon.

- 10 -

Calvin Hughes spent the next morning packing his tent and gear and stowing it in the stable at the burned-out relay station. He saddled his spare horse, tucking the ledgers he'd found with the busted safe into his saddlebags, and he pushed Sequoia out in front of him with just a harness and coiled lead, riding west toward the Santa Rita mine.

He arrived at the mine and tied both horses near Cushman's tent, but the foreman wasn't anywhere to be found.

"I think he rode over to Fort Bayard," one of the men at the camp told him. "Said he needed to send a telegram."

Over by the mess hall, Hughes saw the two Pinkerton guards. They were washed and had on fresh clothes now, but their change of clothes were still dark suits. They also looked like men who had appreciated a good night's sleep and late in the morning were just sitting down to their breakfasts. They sat at a table set up in a clearing down below the mess hall. A big juniper gave them shade from the sun, but as Hughes walked up the two men were lifting the table to move it out of the shade, having decided the warmth of the morning sun was more valuable to them than the lack of glare provided by the juniper.

"Mind if I join you?" Hughes asked.

"Pull up a chair," Woods said. "I think there's still food in the mess hall."

"I've eaten," Hughes said, though he'd only had some jerky and a dry biscuit. "More interested in conversation than food."

Woods gave Hughes a suspicious glance.

"What do you want to talk about?"

"I'm interested in how the search went with the posse, what you saw and didn't see. Interested to know why the two of you continued your pursuit after the troopers from Fort Bayard gave up."

Woods shrugged.

"Duty," he said. "We're paid to protect the mine company's payroll."

"And you didn't have any luck tracking down the

Apache?" Hughes asked.

"Like we told you last night. No luck."

The men ate while Hughes talked to them.

"You boys ever track Apache before?" Hughes asked.

Woods nodded and cleared his throat.

"I rode with a posse a year ago after an Apache raid on a little mining camp west of here. They were looking for volunteers because the Apache killed a family up there, and folks were riled up. We tracked them up into the mountains, into the pine forests yonder, and finally caught them down in draw. Punished 'em pretty good."

"Was that with the army?" Hughes asked.

"Soldiers from Fort Bayard, a lot of men from Silver City. Must have been better than a hundred of us."

"I wonder why you caught them a year ago, but didn't catch this bunch," Hughes said.

Woods' eyes bounced around the camp, looking off in lots of different directions while he thought about it.

"Hell, I couldn't say. Truth is, these were easier to track."

"The ones from the relay station?" Hughes asked.

"Yes."

"Why were they easier to track?"

"Well, for one, they took the road. Them Apache from a year ago attacked the cabins at that mining camp, they didn't take a trail you could recognize, not even take a deer path. Tracking them up through the forest was hard

110

work, but our tracker knew his business. But these that attacked the relay station, they followed the road all the way out of the hills and down to the Rio Grande. I imagine a woman on a blind horse could track Apache that take a road."

"I reckon so," Hughes said.

"The ones that attacked the relay station, they were riding shod horses, too. A horse with shoes is far easier to track than one without. The horseshoe will strike a rock and leave a nice, bright blaze that's easy to follow."

"Where'd they get shod horses?" Hughes asked.

"Well, I reckon they stole them from the relay station."

Hughes shook his head.

"I went to Silver City a couple of days ago and talked to Casper Bennett. He says there were not horses missing from the relay station's stock."

"Maybe so," Woods said, shoving a bite of food into his mouth. "He would know better than me."

He chewed his breakfast for a moment, then he swallowed.

"And for another, that Indian scout we had leading us this time, about the only thing he can track is his way to the saloon. He's just a damned drunk. That's why me and Pickens decided to keep scouting the Rio Grande for tracks."

"But you did not find any?"

"Nope. They took the road to the river, but then they did their Apache vanishing trick."

"Who made the decision to abandon the pursuit?"

Hughes asked.

"That lieutenant from the fort," Woods said. "Him and Tucker, the deputy sheriff, they argued about it a good bit. But it was the lieutenant, finally. He said the rest of us could keep running in circles if we wanted, but he and his men were done."

"I guess he made the right decision," Hughes said. "Seeing as how you boys kept at it for a couple of days longer and didn't find anything."

Pickens tossed down his fork and it clanged against the metal plate. He looked peeved.

"Maybe so, maybe not," he said. "Neither one of us is a professional trackers. If they'd brought a damn decent scout, we might be sitting here talking about how we got that payroll money back from the Apache."

"I think that's right," Woods said. "That scout is just a drunk."

Hughes fixed his gaze at a point between the two men. For his next question, he wanted to be able to watch both of them, to see if either reacted.

"Have you considered that maybe it wasn't Apache who did it?"

Pickens took a bite of his breakfast, indifferent. Woods sniffed as he thought for a moment.

"It had to be Apache," he said. "The stagecoach driver saw them."

Hughes thanked the men and left them to finish their breakfast in peace. He mounted the spare horse and pushed Sequoia out in front of him. Along the way he passed Cushman, returning already from Fort Bayard. Both men drew reins as they came level with each other on the road.

"Any luck finding that money yet?" Cushman asked.

"None yet," Hughes said.

"Well, I haven't lost my job yet," he said. "Had a telegram from St. Louis, and all they said was that the payroll would be coming in the next week or so."

"Glad for you," Hughes said.

"Have y'all tracked down Robinson and McCay yet?" Cushman asked.

Hughes furrowed his brow.

"I'm afraid I don't know Robinson and McCay."

"Your woman friend wanted to talk to them when she was out here yesterday. I sent for them down in the mine, but they rode off without talking to her."

"Is that right?" Hughes said. "I haven't seen Miss Blake, so I couldn't say if she's tracked them or not."

"Well, they never did come back to work. I don't know what their trouble is."

Hughes scratched at his chin.

"I'll let Miss Blake know when I see her."

"Sooner you find that money, the happier I'll be," Cushman told him. "I'd feel a mite more comfortable about keeping my job if I could tell them in St. Louis that the lost payroll has been recovered."

- 11 -

Hughes tied both horses on posts outside the saloon at Fort Bayard, and he walked inside. The saloon's windows were all shuttered against the chill of the morning air, and a stove against the wall put off too much heat so that the air was dry. Hughes rubbed his eyes with finger and thumb. Several lanterns inside the saloon were burning, and there was light enough to easily find the half-breed scout, Yuyutsu. "Apache Tom," is what Corporal Greaves said they called him. Finding him was all that much easier, too, because only Apache Tom and a bartender were in the saloon.

"Morning," the bartender said. "You looking for breakfast or a drink?"

"I'll take a cup of coffee," Hughes said.

The bartender frowned. There wasn't much profit in serving coffee in a bar, but he poured a mug full of black water and put it in front of Hughes. The Wells Fargo man tasted the coffee and made a face at it.

"What's the matter?" the bartender asked, almost daring Hughes to insult the coffee.

"It tastes like you've flavored it with cow chips," Hughes remarked.

"Order whiskey next time if you don't like the coffee."

Hughes was standing about halfway down the bar. Apache Tom was sitting at one end of the bar. He had a beer and a shot of whiskey in front of him.

"Morning," Hughes said to him.

Apache Tom turned his head and gave Hughes an appraising look.

"You're not with the army."

"No," Hughes said. "I'm not with the army."

"What do you want?"

"I want to know what you can tell me about the Apache you tracked," Hughes said.

Hughes introduced himself. The tracker remained indifferent, sipping at his whiskey as Hughes spoke.

"I'm trying to find the men who murdered the station workers."

"I tried to find them, too. They doubled back in the river, hiding their tracks. I could not find where they left the river. I do not know where they are."

"Were they Apache?" Hughes asked.

"Of course they were Apache," the tracker said. "The stagecoach man saw them ride away."

"Did they look like Apache tracks?" Hughes asked.

Apache Tom narrowed his eyes.

"What are you saying?"

"I'm not saying anything," Hughes said. "I'm just trying to find out. Did you think, when you were following those tracks, that it was Apache you were chasing?"

"Of course," Apache Tom said. "Who else would it be?"

"Anybody else," Hughes said.

"Do you ask because the horses wore shoes? Apache can ride shod horses the same as anyone else."

Right away Hughes said that he wouldn't get anywhere with this man. The army scout was almost hostile about being questioned. Hughes could not say if the man's professional pride caused the hostility, or if it was something else.

"I'm just asking because I'd like to get your thoughts," Hughes said.

"I did not see the riders. Maybe they were Apache. Maybe they were not. I followed the tracks. The tracks were left by horses."

Hughes chuckled, though there was no mirth in the

half-breed's joke.

"Okay then," Hughes said. "Thanks for your time."

He decided not to finish his coffee and instead left the full mug sitting on the bar. Hughes walked outside and unlashed the horses from the posts. He tightened the cinch on the saddle, and while he did, he noticed the second lieutenant who'd led the posse walking up the road. Hughes lowered his head so that his face was obscured by the brim of his hat. The lieutenant paid him no attention. The man walked with a singular purpose, long strides taking him toward the saloon.

Hughes tried to remember — Lucy had used the lieutenant's name. Stellman? He thought that was right.

Stellman stepped into the saloon and pulled the door closed behind him. Hughes left the horses and stepped over to one of the windows. The shutter on the window was cracked just a bit, and Hughes opened it up a touch so that he could see inside where the second lieutenant and the Indian scout were already engaged in a heated conversation. The barman had moved away from them. Hughes could not hear what they were saying because they kept their voices low, but both men appeared angry.

Out in California, the Wells Fargo agent had ridden with posses that included cavalry troopers and Indian scouts. He'd never known any of the Indian scouts particularly well, but he'd observed their interactions with army officers. Most often, the Indians scouts kept a professional distance between them and the army men they worked for. What Hughes could never remember seeing was a scout taking an angry posture toward an officer, not even a second lieutenant.

But there was no doubt now that Stellman and

Apache Tom were engaged in a heated exchange and that each man was giving as good as he got.

In his career as a Wells Fargo man, Calvin Hughes had learned to accept that sometimes he encountered things he did not understand and it was best to just mark those things in his mind. Usually, they would come back around.

***

All that Fort Bayard had to offer in the way of rooms to let could be found inside a couple of boarding houses, and neither of the owners had Lucy Blake and Albert Fears staying in any of their rooms. So Hughes rode the horses back out to the road and continued west, heading for Silver City. The road climbed up and over rolling hills, down again into little creek valleys where snakes of willows and cottonwoods marked the place where the water ran in the wet months, and across wide swaths dotted with juniper. Whether perceptible or not, the altitude was always climbing, taking Hughes higher up toward the distant mountains.

Silver City sat at the precipice, lower down than the camp where he'd found the stolen safe, but quite a bit higher than the Santa Rita mine – which itself felt lofty compared to the Rio Grande valley.

The city started its life after silver ore deposits were discovered nearby. It began as a tent city erected along streets John Bullard laid out on his farm.

In the intervening decade, Silver City established two reputations, seemingly along polar lines. Sheriff Whitehill and his deputies, Dangerous Dan Tucker among them, were known to be rough and ready lawmen who never hesitated to clear leather. But a boy known as "the Kid" who was currently making a reputation as a bad man for himself over in Lincoln also got his start killing folks in Silver City.

Hughes rode into Silver City on the back of his spare horse. When he pulled reins out front of the Wells Fargo office, Sequoia stopped and waited for him.

"You're back," Casper Bennett observed from behind his desk.

"I was hoping I could put my horses in your corral," Hughes said. "Maybe for the day, maybe for a couple of days."

"You can do that," Casper said. "Have you learned anything more?"

Hughes shrugged his shoulders. If he had, he wouldn't have told Casper Bennett. Not yet, anyway.

"I've learned a little, but not enough to say any more than I did when I was here a couple of days ago. I do have a question for you, though. If I was a single woman traveling with a male companion, which hotel would I be likely to stay in?"

Casper Bennett narrowed his eyes.

"Would you be a single woman with an eye patch?"

Hughes grinned at him.

"You've met my friend."

"She came around here yesterday afternoon with a big, mean-looking fellow."

"He's not so mean," Hughes said. "Not when you

get to know him."

"Well, he didn't make himself known. Never even introduced himself. The woman did all the talking. She said they're Pinkerton detectives. Said they were traveling with you, but that they'd left you back at your camp."

"I'm aiming to find them now," Hughes said.

"The Palace Hotel," Casper Bennett said. "I told them to go to the Palace Hotel. Four blocks down on Broadway Street. It's a new building, two-stories. Nice courtyard around back. You won't miss it."

"The Palace Hotel," Hughes repeated.

The sun had grown warm, and Hughes now stripped out of his duster and his coat. He hung them on hooks near the door.

"Mind if I stow these here?" he asked.

"Help yourself," Casper said.

He had half a mind to let Casper Bennett look at the ledgers he'd found in the mining camp up north. Bennett might be able to provide some insight – discover some anomaly in the deposits and withdrawals or notice an unusual notation from his uncle. But Calvin Hughes had not decided if Casper Bennett might have had some role in what happened out at the relay station. He was one of the few who knew how much money Roy Bennett handled at that relay station. It was an unusual situation, a stagecoach relay station holding an entire mining operation's payroll. No random thief or gang of road agents would even suspect such a prize at a relay station.

So until Hughes had decided for sure that Bennett wasn't involved, he was reluctant to seek his advice with the ledgers.

"My experience is that oftentimes in a robbery situation there is someone running the show," Hughes said, just idly talking as Casper Bennett sat behind his desk. Bennett looked up, furrowing his brow as if disinclined to hear Hughes' interruption. "Usually someone smart enough to plan out a robbery, but also smart enough not to get involved in the actual doing of the thing."

"That makes sense," Bennett said.

"He plans out the robbery and then partners up with a gang to actually go and commit the robbery. It gives him some sense of security against prosecution. He has an alibi, you understand. At the time of the robbery, he's at a restaurant dining in front of two dozen witnesses."

"Sure," Bennett said, distracted with whatever papers he had on his desk.

"But sometimes, I would even say most often, it's the man who plans the robbery who gets the most time in prison."

Casper Bennett looked up from his distraction.

"Why is that?" he asked.

"Most often, the men we catch first are the ones who commit the act. Either we track them from the scene or we find them with the stolen money. And that first man we catch, he almost always cuts a deal. Less prison time, sometimes he walks away without even being charged if he testifies against the others in his gang. And the first man he squeals on is the man who planned the robbery."

"I suppose that makes some sense," Casper Bennett said. "I guess it begs the question, though. How close are you to catching the first man?"

Hughes gave a small shrug and grinned at the man.

"Probably closer than he knows."

There was no truth in it. Unless Lucy Blake had uncovered something, Hughes had no confidence that they were getting close at all. He had no true suspects. He walked out of the Wells Fargo office, leaving Casper Bennett, and started down Broadway toward the Palace Hotel where he hoped he would find Lucy Blake and Albert Fears.

Cushman at the mine knew about the payroll money, but so did everyone else at the mine.

Casper Bennett remained as much a suspect as anyone else. He had knowledge of the relay station, its workings, and the money in the safe.

Hughes had decided the two Pinkerton men, Pickens and Woods, were unlikely suspects, but he could not rule them out, either.

Hughes did not know anything about the men Robinson and Blake who Cushman said had ridden away when Lucy was attempting to interview them. Maybe they were suspects.

The lieutenant, Stellman, at Fort Bayard bothered Hughes. Something was not right about that man, and Hughes' skeptical nature made him suspect that Stellman and the scout Apache Tom were involved in something. But he did not know what that was, and it seemed unlikely that either of them were tied up in the robbery at the relay station.

Any of them might be involved, Hughes conceded.

Or none of them. It might be that the men responsible for the robbery and murder at the relay station had fled the area. They could easily be in Arizona territory, or even California by now. They might have headed north, gone to Colorado or Utah. They'd had time enough now that they could be to the Mississippi River, for that matter. They could have ridden to Mesilla or even up to Albuquerque and boarded a train by now.

A sign over the door identified the Palace Hotel, but Hughes did not need the sign to find it. In the courtyard, sitting at a picnic table in the shade of a willow tree, Lucy Blake was calling to him.

- 12 -

"Robinson and McCay," Lucy said firmly.

After Hughes secured a room for himself at the Palace Hotel, he and Lucy Blake sat under the willow tree in the small courtyard of the Palace Hotel. The hotel took up the entirety of the corner block at Broadway and Bullard, and along the side of the building on Bullard there was a narrow courtyard running the length of the hotel. Tables and chairs were positioned in shady spots under shrubs or the lone willow tree. The courtyard clearly had been designed to take advantage of the existing tree. It was there, with a decent breeze cutting through the streets of the town and the willow providing shade, that Hughes and Lucy Blake compared notes on what they had learned separately.

Hughes told Lucy about following the wagon tracks to an abandoned prospecting camp north of Silver City. He told her about the safe and ledgers he'd recovered. He told her about meeting the two Pinkerton guards from the mine.

And now it was Lucy's turn to share what she knew.

"Mark my words. Robinson and McCay are going to be our men. They work at the mine. They would have known there were two months' payroll in the relay station safe. The day of the attack they took a wagon, supposedly to help the camp's cook fetch supplies. But he said he went to Fort Bayard for supplies and returned alone. Cushman sent someone into the mine to fetch them so that I could talk to them, and instead of coming to talk to me, the two of them hightailed it out of there."

"When I met Cushman on the road this morning, he told me they'd not returned to the mine," Hughes said, agreeing it all sounded very suspicious. "Any line on where they are?"

"Mr. Fears is working on that now," Lucy said. "After we got rooms here last night, Mr. Fears went around to some of the saloons asking for them. He met a man who said two men from the mine rode into town yesterday on lathered horses. This man Mr. Fears spoke to, he works at the livery stable where McCay and Robinson left their horses. As of about two hours ago, the horses were still there. Mr. Fears is keeping a watch on that stable now."

Hughes checked his watch. It was late in the afternoon, but there was still time left in the day.

"Let's walk down to the Western Union office," he said. "If Robinson and McCay are known outlaws, maybe James Hume can help us."

Lucy wore a dark walking skirt and white blouse with a rust-colored vest buttoned over the blouse. She wore her hair up with a small hat pinned to her hair with a tuft of lace attached to it. The hat did nothing to keep the sun out of her eyes, and in a rainstorm would be worthless, but Hughes suspected it was a fashionable sort of hat and that she did not wear it for utility purposes. She looked smart on the streets of Silver City, where some number of the women were prostitutes and a fair portion of the others looked like they spent their time swinging a pickax with their husbands. In fact, as they walked down the street, Lucy with her arm inside Calvin Hughes' elbow the way she liked to do, Hughes could feel the eyes of the folks they passed lingering on them. It might be that Lucy Blake was as pretty as any woman who walked the streets of Silver City, but almost as an afterthought – because he'd become accustomed to it – Hughes realized they probably earned the stares through Lucy's eye patch. The eye patch, along with the scar and the fine clothes, gave her a mysterious sort of air.

"People are staring at us," Hughes mumbled to Lucy, and he felt himself stand up a bit straighter under their looks.

"It's probably because you're so handsome," Lucy said with a small laugh.

The telegram went to James B. Hume at his San Francisco office. It was a simple message asking for information on Josh Robinson and Daniel McCay. Hughes told the Western Union man to deliver any reply to the Palace Hotel, and on the way back there they decided to stroll past the livery stable to check on Albert Fears. They found Fears leaning against the wall of a building across from the livery.

"I checked when I got here, and the man in the stable said Robinson and McCay haven't been back for their horses," Fears said. "If they intend to ride out on those horses, they're still in Silver City."

"If they don't intend to ride out on those horses, we'd better be watching to see who boards tomorrow morning's stagecoach," Hughes said.

Hughes and Lucy Blake took a seat on a bench under an awning in front of a store across from the livery and gave Albert Fears a respite to go and get himself some supper. They chatted idly, keeping in mind that they might be overheard and so careful not to discuss the little they'd learned so far about the murder and robbery at the relay station nor to talk about their suspicions. When anyone is a suspect, everyone is dangerous.

So instead of discussing anything that mattered, Lucy suggested that they get dinner at a restaurant down the street from the Palace Hotel. She told Hughes about a dress she'd ordered from a catalog and wondered out loud if it had arrived in Albuquerque and would be there when they got home.

And all the while, they watched the livery stable for Robinson and McCay. Lucy would not recognize the men – all she'd seen was the two men ride away. But one of the horses they'd left on was a black mare, and Lucy was sure she would recognize the horse. But it did not matter. No one left the livery while they sat there, and only one man rode in to leave a horse.

When Fears returned, Lucy and Hughes went to get

supper together. Fears said he would watch the livery until dark, assuming the men would not be likely to flee the city in the night.

After supper, a telegram was waiting for Hughes at the Palace Hotel.

"Let's go up to my room," Hughes suggested, not wanting to read or discuss the telegram in public.

They hurried up the steps to the second-floor landing and down the hall to Hughes' room. Inside, Hughes tore open the envelope and scanned the telegram from Hume.

"Joshua Robinson and Daniel McCay were both involved in two Wells Fargo stagecoach robberies in Arizona Territory. They were arrested with two accomplices, but all four escaped jail. The other two were recaptured, tried and convicted. Both of them are in the Yuma prison. Robinson and McCay are still wanted."

"That's it," Lucy Blake said, a smile crossing her face. "Do I win the bet?"

Hughes laughed.

"I believe the bet was the first to recover the money."

Lucy frowned at him.

"Will we not go together to arrest them?" she asked.

Hughes shrugged.

"We might."

"Then surely the one who first identified the suspects is the winner of the bet."

Hughes folded the telegram and stuck it in his pocket.

"I'll take you and Mr. Fears on a picnic," Hughes conceded. "But first we've got to catch these men."

- 13 -

"Lucy, a woman with an eye patch is hard to miss," Hughes said, his tone gave away his frustration. "You go and find Deputy Tucker. And while you do, Mr. Fears and I will watch the stagecoach."

First thing that morning, under the auspices of retrieving his coat and duster, Hughes returned to the Wells Fargo office. Without outright asking, he wanted to learn if Robinson and McCay intended to be on it. The morning coach ran from Silver City to Mesilla. If Robinson and McCay boarded that stagecoach for Mesilla, they could be in El Paso in three days, and in El Paso, they could board a train that could take them anywhere they wanted to go this side of Europe. In a week they could be in Canada or Mexico, on a boat to the Far East or in New York City. And, likely as not, neither Wells Fargo nor the Pinkerton Detective Agency would ever apprehend the men.

So Hughes made small talk with Casper Bennett after he took his coat and duster from the pegs at the door, asking about the manifest for the morning's coach and then idly asking about the passengers. Though irritated with the questions, Bennett readily offered the information that two men traveling together had purchased tickets to Mesilla the day before.

"How soon does the coach leave?" Hughes asked.

But even as he spoke, the driver and shotgun rider for the stagecoach were arriving from the boarding house where they spent the night, and a couple of Wells Fargo men was harnessing the stagecoach outside.

"It'll leave in thirty minutes," Bennett said.

Hughes was half tempted to enlist the shotgun rider's help and apprehend the two men himself, but the jehu was leaning against the counter and the shotgun rider had taken a seat on the bench in the Wells Fargo office, and Hughes could not risk saying anything to either man. Not in front of Casper Bennett.

Robinson and McCay may well have been involved in the robbery and murder at the relay station, but so were other people. The way Hughes counted it, no less than six men had to have been involved. Four men, dressed as Apache, rode away from the stagecoach when it appeared on the hill over the relay station. But someone else left with the safe. They stole a wagon from the relay station and toted the stolen safe to the abandoned mining camp beside a mountain river north of Silver City. That would have taken no less than two men.

Robinson and McCay might be two of the six, but if they were involved in the relay station robbery, they had accomplices, and Calvin Hughes had not yet eliminated Casper Bennett as a possible accomplice.

So he hurried back to the Palace Hotel.

"The stagecoach will leave on time," Hughes said again to Lucy Blake. "And we're running out of time, now. They'll set out for Mesilla in fifteen minutes. You go and find Deputy Tucker and bring him quickly to the Wells Fargo office. Mr. Fears and I will apprehend Robinson and McCay."

Lucy squinted her eye at him and angrily pursed her lips, but at last she nodded.

"All right, then," Lucy agreed, reluctantly. "I'll go and fetch the deputy."

Hughes turned to Albert Fears who simply nodded.

"Lead the way," Fears said.

Hughes took the stairs in the Palace Hotel two at a time and was out the door in flash. Fears, breathing heavily, jogged not far behind him. For all his size, Albert Fears managed to remain surprisingly athletic.

They were only a few blocks from the Wells Fargo office, and Hughes slowed his jog to a quick walk when he came within sight of the stagecoach. Albert Fears caught him there, and both men now walked, taking long strides.

"They're loading the luggage," Fears said, and Hughes could see it, too. The jehu was up on the top of the stagecoach while the shotgun rider and Casper Bennett handed up luggage to him.

A small throng of people had gathered round the stagecoach, as they always did. Passengers ready to board the coach, loved ones and friends there to see them off. Hughes knew, from his conversation with Casper, that in addition to the two men traveling together the stagecoach's passenger list included a local gambler who often traveled between Silver City and Mesilla, the widow of a prospector, recently killed in an accident, who intended to return home to her people back East and an old timer who'd just made a small fortune after hitting on a silver claim and then selling it to a big outfit funded by investors in New York City.

"Nobody's aboard yet," Hughes said. "If they see us coming and they're feeling skittish, you can bet they'll take off. I'd rather take these men alive if we can safely do it."

"If I can get close enough to lay hands on one of them, I can take him alive," Albert Fears said confidently. "He could be a little banged up, but he'll be alive."

They were a block away now, and across the road from the Wells Fargo office. The jehu was still atop the stagecoach, pulling a rope taut as he strapped down the luggage. No one had yet boarded the coach.

Hughes scanned the faces in the crowd, trying to pick out the two who were Robinson and McCay. They were all standing along the boardwalk and in the road at the back of the coach.

Several women stood nearby to see off the prospector's widow. She was a young woman, and as his eyes ran across her, Hughes thought in that half-second that she was young enough and pretty enough that she would probably find a second husband back home. Three women stood around her, all four of them looked like they had just come from church. There was hugging and tears as they bid her goodbye.

The old-timer who'd sold off his claim was easy to spot. Bent at the back but wearing a new suit and leaning on a polished cane, he didn't look like he'd live long to enjoy his earnings. Hughes wondered if he had heirs. He stood against his cane by himself, not even a drinking buddy to see him off.

The gambler sat on a bench in front of the Wells Fargo office. His clothes were clean and fresh looking, his boots had a shine. He was idly picking his teeth – an accustomed traveler just waiting for the activity to be done so he could board the coach.

A boy with a sack of mail also stood by. The mail would go inside the coach with the passengers. Another man stood on the boardwalk, one foot propped up on a large trunk, his elbows resting against his knee. He seemed to be watching without really seeing the work the Wells Fargo men were doing. He was waiting his turn. Whatever he was shipping in the trunk would soon be strapped onto the back of the stagecoach when the jehu was finished with the lighter-weight luggage up on top.

In front of the man with the trunk, both of them standing off the boardwalk and on the dirt street, two men stood close to each other, adopting a posture that suggested they were whispering. One of the men even had his hand up covering his mouth as he tilted his head toward the other.

They wore worn and wrinkled clothes. Their shirts were patched at the elbows and their trousers patched at the knees. The morning sun revealed upon their coats a layer of grime. Their hats were dirty, and Hughes could even see a couple of pieces of straw stuck to them that suggested they'd spent the night in a hayloft.

Now Hughes and Fears were level with the lead horses of the stagecoach team, and Hughes glanced over his shoulder to be sure he had a clear path to start across the street in a diagonal that would take them directly to the two men at the back of the stagecoach.

"Those are going to be our two boys, right there," Hughes said, a subtle head nod toward the men.

Subtle or not, Robinson and McCay noticed Hughes and Fears coming toward them, and they had no misgivings about the men's intentions.

Without warning, both McCay and Robinson spun on their heels and started to run.

"Tarnation!" Albert Fears swore, but Hughes gave chase.

Josh Robinson turned and ran right down the middle of Main Street. Hughes followed him.

Albert Fears started after Dan McCay, but it was a lost cause before the thing even got fully started. McCay went for the corral where they kept the stagecoach horses. He hit the corral at a run, planting a hand on the top rail and throwing his legs up and over.

Fears shouted for him to stop, but McCay ignored the shouts. McCay darted across the corral, dodging the horses that wandered into his way, and he went over the rails on the far side almost as fast as he'd entered the corral.

Fears opted not to try to railing, and instead gave his pursuit around the corral. On the far side it opened up on Bullard Street, as crowded with shops and homes as Main Street.

It happened that the Wells Fargo corral was a common cut-through from Bullard to Main, and as McCay went over the top rail to exit the corral, he spotted the woman with the eye patch entering the corral's lot from Bullard Street. She was walking with a man McCay knew well.

Everyone in Silver City and the surrounding area knew Dangerous Dan Tucker.

Not long ago, a drunken Mexican was standing on the street throwing rocks at people. Someone ran to get the sheriff's deputy to deal with the man. Tucker rounded the corner, saw the drunken Mexican with a handful of rocks, and without warning or any preamble, Tucker drew his six-shooter and shot the man in the neck, killing him almost before he hit the ground.

Lucy Blake saw the man leap over the railing and out of the corral. She heard Albert Fears shouting, and she followed his voice until she saw him running around the corral, his eyes fixed on the fleeing suspect.

"Deputy Tucker," Lucy said. "You should stop that man."

Dangerous Dan didn't need to be told twice.

With his thumbnail, he flipped the leather thong off the hammer of his six-gun and in the space of a heartbeat he'd snatched the gun from its holster.

The shot was about twenty yards, and the target was moving.

"Don't kill him!" Lucy gasped, realizing that Dan

Tucker intended to shoot, but her plea disappeared in the concussion of the gun.

The lead bullet caught McCay in the hip, and he went down with a scream and a cloud of dust.

Josh Robinson ran up Main Street. The man had a burly torso, built almost like a barrel, from swinging a sledgehammer at the mine. He was strong as an ox. But he wasn't built for an extended foot chase. He had enough of a jump on Hughes that it seemed unlikely the Wells Fargo man would catch him. But Robinson quickly felt the burning in his thighs. His breathing was coming fast, so fast that he struggled to get any air into his lungs. And he knew he was slowing down. And he could hear the man in pursuit, his breathing, growing louder, was also heavy, but it was steady.

And Hughes was beginning to catch Robinson, closing the distance.

The Wells Fargo man did not shout. He wanted to save his breath.

And then Josh Robinson's left foot dropped down into a pothole in the road. His ankle turned in a way it shouldn't have. And Josh Robinson found his momentum was carrying his face toward the ground and his feet were flinging over his head.

Hughes jerked his heavy Schofield from its holster, and he threw himself knee-first into Josh Robinson's back. Whatever breath the man still had in his body, Hughes knocked it all out. Then he cracked the barrel of the Schofield over the man's skull, rendering him senseless.

***

Jeff Robinson sat in a chair inside the Silver City jail house, his wrists bound in iron behind his back, his head spinning.

"Who helped you at the relay station?" Dan Tucker asked. His voice was gravely and menacing, but no more menacing that his cold eyes. "You tell me what I want to know, and maybe you won't find yourself swinging from the scaffold."

Robinson could not think straight.

The woman with the eye patch and the man who'd clubbed him with the gun barrel stood behind Dan Tucker, but it was the deputy who was near to him, their faces so close that Robinson could feel the man's breath against his own face.

"Nobody helped us," Robinson said.

"Somebody helped you," Calvin Hughes said. "The two of you didn't make off with a safe and pretend to be four Apache Indians."

Robinson shook his head.

"That wasn't us," he said. "We never did rob the relay station."

"You left the mine the day of the robbery," Lucy Blake said. "You took a wagon, but you did not go to Fort Bayard for supplies."

Robinson nodded his head, feeling the throbbing grow worse.

"I admit it, we went to the stagecoach station to rob it," Robinson said. "We knew there were two months of payroll up there in the safe, and we were sick of slinging hammers all day. But we never did steal that safe. We were going to wait for the stagecoach to leave. We drove the wagon off into the brush to hide it, and then we went down to the relay station to keep a watch. We figured as soon as the stagecoach left, we'd ride in there and take the money. If they wouldn't open the safe, we had the wagon and we figured we could take the whole thing."

"But you didn't do it?" Tucker asked.

"When we got to the relay station, there were a gang of Apache. They'd already killed the two men, and they were loading the safe on a wagon."

Lucy turned to look at Cal Hughes, who turned to look at her. Dan Tucker stood up and paced a turn or two in the room.

Hughes chewed his lip.

"You're headed to Yuma," Hughes said. "You're wanted for two stagecoach robberies, and for fleeing incarceration in Arizona. You're looking at a long sentence, Robinson. Twenty years, maybe. You'll be an old man before you get out of there. Make it easy on yourself. Tell us the truth about the relay station. We know it wasn't Apache."

Robinson shook his head again and winced at the pain. He was wearing a dark stubble on his face and bags under his eyes. He looked like a hunted man, haggard and downtrodden.

"I was there," he said. "That's what I'm telling you. Me and Dan, we saw them."

"How close were you?" Hughes asked.

"Up on the western hill above the stagecoach station," Robinson said.

"If you didn't have anything to do with the robbery at the relay station, then why did you run when Miss Blake came to talk to you at the mine day before yesterday?" Hughes asked.

"Because we're wanted in Arizona Territory," Robinson said. Then he changed the subject. "How is Dan?"

Hughes glanced over at Deputy Tucker, still pacing the small room.

"He's with a doctor now," Tucker said.

While true enough, Tucker also put a happier face on it than perhaps it deserved. The bullet smashed the man's pelvic bone and tore him apart in the lower abdomen. The doctor predicted a small chance of survive and administered enough morphine that Dan McCay went to sleep. Albert Fears stood guard over the injured man, though there was no need to worry that he might still try to make an escape. Even if he had the strength, his injuries were such that he would never walk again. Lucy Blake told Fears to be alert in case the man woke up and decided to make a deathbed confession.

Through the morning, the interview with Robinson continued in similar fashion.

Robinson readily confessed that he and McCay cooked up a plan to steal the mine's payroll from the Wells Fargo relay station, but he steadfastly maintained his lack of guilt. All he'd done was watch from the hill above the relay station.

He insisted he'd seen Apache, and that it was the Indians off the reservation who'd committed the crime.

In his frustration, Hughes finally said to the man, "Give up the names of the others, tell us where the money is, and I'll see to it you never spend a day in prison – not for this and not for what you've done in Arizona."

But Robinson continue to stick to the same story.

They'd been at it for more than three hours – Hughes did the questioning; then Tucker did the questioning; then Lucy Blake made the man tell the entire story all over again. Finally, the three lawmen stepped outside of the jail house and had a discussion among themselves.

"His story isn't changing," Dan Tucker said.

"And he seems to be telling the truth," Lucy Blake observed.

Hughes nodded his head. He typically could get a good read on people and trusted his own judgment. Josh Robinson did seem to be telling the truth.

"It's an awfully big coincidence that he and McCay went to the relay station to steal from it on the very same day that someone else raided the relay station," Hughes said.

Lucy gave a small shrug of her shoulders, as if she did not think it was that big of a coincidence.

"It would be a coincidence if was a band of renegade Apache off the reservation," she said. "But if it was someone who knew about the payroll, the same as Robinson and McCay, then maybe it's not that much of a coincidence. Two months' worth of payroll in the safe. We figured that's around six thousand dollars. That's a sizable prize."

Tucker glanced from Lucy Blake to Calvin Hughes.

"The two of you are operating on the assumption

this was not Apache?"

"That's our assumption," Hughes confirmed.

"But the stagecoach driver said it was," Tucker said. "And if we believe Robinson, he confirms it."

Hughes shrugged and made a tisking click with his tongue.

"It doesn't take much to dress up like an Apache," Hughes said. "The only men who saw those raiders up close are dead now – Bennett and Thacker. The stagecoach men – and Robinson if we believe him – were all some distance away, at least fifty or sixty yards by my reckoning, and maybe closer to a hundred."

Tucker scratched at his chin.

"What do you want done with Robinson?" he asked.

"Hold him. I'll wire San Francisco, but I expect they'll send someone to take him to Arizona. McCay, too, if he survives."

- 14 -

Calvin Hughes had a sense that his time was running out.

He couldn't explain it, exactly. But he knew the feeling – an urgency that crept over him during an investigation and made him know that if he did not soon solve his case, he would lose the opportunity to solve it. Even though he did not show up in Silver City until days after the robbery, he'd not yet felt like time was getting thin on him. But now he felt it.

He stood alone now in the courtyard of the Palace

Hotel smoking a Buchanan & Lyall cigar and thinking about what he knew.

Before leaving Josh Robinson at the jail house, Hughes tried one more time, dangling freedom in front of the condemned man.

"Turn on your accomplices, and you'll never spend a minute of time in prison," Hughes told him.

But still the man refused to come off his story.

So Hughes and Blake gave up. Tucker put Robinson in the jail to hold him until a Wells Fargo agent could come to collect Robinson, and maybe McCay.

Cushman seemed an unlikely suspect. They had no evidence he was even away from the mine the day of the robbery.

Casper Bennett likewise seemed an unlikely suspect. Nothing about the man so far suggested he was anything other than a thorough express man. And beyond that, he gave no indication that he was the sort of man who would kill his own uncle – an uncle who had helped secure him good employment – for a few thousand dollars.

"What are you doing down there?" Lucy Blake called from above.

Hughes turned to look back at the Palace Hotel, and saw Lucy leaning out of her open window on the second floor.

"Feeling like we should hurry," Hughes said.

Lucy was smiling down at him. For a brief moment, Hughes had thought the two of them might strike up a romance. But that had not happened, not yet. Instead, they'd settled into a friendly professional relationship that involved some heavy flirtation and nothing more. But he was hopeful. He had a soft spot for beautiful women, and even with the scar on her cheek and the eye patch over her eye, Lucy Blake remained as attractive as any woman Hughes had ever met.

"Are you that hungry? Give me a few minutes to change clothes and freshen up, and then we'll go," Lucy said.

"Not hurry to dinner," Hughes said. As they often did at home in Albuquerque, Hughes and Lucy had decided to get supper together and he was in the courtyard waiting for her. "Hurry and catch the men who committed the robbery at the relay station."

Lucy frowned.

"You think we're running out of time?" she asked.

"Maybe it's the fact that Robinson and McCay were trying to leave town on the stagecoach this morning, but yes, I think we're running out of time. If the men who did this are still in town, I don't think they will be for long."

Lucy nodded. "I'll be down in a minute."

She disappeared inside the window, and Hughes turned back toward the street, taking another long draw on his cigar.

Evening cast a soft light on the town, filtering down through the willow trees planted along the street to give shade in the summer. The trees were not yet particularly tall, but they'd probably been growing for nearly a decade, and they were beginning to reach a height where they would serve their intended purpose.

Though not crowded, the boardwalk definitely now

had more people than were out during the day. A chilly breeze cut down through the street as night descended, and Hughes knew the evening would turn cold.

He leaned against the brick wall of the courtyard, rolling his cigar between his fingers and running through his mind the details of the relay station robbery. He was not yet fully prepared to release Robinson and McCay as suspects. If there were at least four other men on the loose, Robinson might be unwilling to name them in the hopes that they would make some effort to break him from jail. After all, Robinson and McCay had escaped custody once already.

Hughes was deep in the process of convincing himself that Robinson and McCay were still likely suspects when a commotion down the road caught his attention.

At first, he thought it was a simple matter of a few drunken prospectors getting too rowdy. Several men stepped down off the high boardwalk – built tall to spare the buildings along Bullard Street from the floods that swept through town during the rainy season. They were out front of a saloon, and the men were clearly too far in their drink for decent behavior.

But when he squinted into the dimming light, Hughes realized the men out front of the saloon, whooping loudly and slapping thighs, were all Negro men, and a couple of them wore cavalry britches. He reasoned they all must be Buffalo Soldiers from Fort Bayard, on leave for the week, maybe. They'd started their drinking early that day and had made the most of it.

In a moment, Hughes learned what the shouting was all about. Three big white men followed them out of the saloon, and as Hughes watched, one of the white men squared off with one of the soldiers. Now several more people walked out of the saloon, and they had a large crowd forming up to watch the brewing fight.

The soldier readying for combat was a big man himself, the biggest of the six soldiers.

As Hughes watched, the white man stepped in for a jab, and the soldier deftly side stepped the punch and grabbed the white man by the arm. Now the boxing match turned quickly into a wrestling event as the two men went into the street in a heap. Both of them were now landing blows on each other.

The actual fight lasted only a few moments – certainly less than a full minute – for someone beyond the crowd whom Hughes could not see raised up a six-shooter and fired a shot into the air.

Dangerous Dan Tucker's reputation, and one shot from his six-shooter, did the job to clear the crowd. The other soldiers, possibly worried that a white deputy would go to work on a bunch of Negro soldiers first, scattered quickly, and not together. They darted down alleyways and along the thoroughfare. One man ran past Hughes where he stood outside the Palace Hotel.

Most of the others who'd followed the fight outside the saloon scurried back inside.

The two combatants, still locked in each other's grips on the ground, became victims of Dan Tucker's wrath. He kicked the men several times and then began bashing them with the grip of his gun.

Hughes watched as Deputy Tucker dragged first one man and then the other to their feet and began leading them down the street toward the jail.

"I'm ready," Lucy Blake said, stepping down into the

courtyard from the side door of the hotel.

She startled him – he'd not heard her coming through the door – and Hughes jumped slightly.

"Did I scare you?" Lucy asked playfully.

"Not hardly," Hughes said. "Just lost in thought. I just watched Dan Tucker break up a fight."

"Did he shoot someone?" Lucy asked darkly.

"No, I think the deputy is limiting his shootings to one person a day. He just bashed these two."

* * *

After supper, Calvin Hughes and Lucy Blake sat on the patio, Lucy sipping from a glass of sherry and Hughes drinking bourbon and smoking a cigar. Albert Fears had returned from his vigil at Dan McCay's deathbed, for that's what it turned out to be.

"He never woke up after they gave him the morphine," Fears said. "Never made any kind of confession."

Hughes was not surprised that McCay didn't make it. Dan Tucker's bullet had smashed the man's hip bone, busting it and wreaking havoc inside McCay's abdomen. That was not the sort of wound a man was likely to survive, and if he did survive it, he'd be terribly maimed for whatever portion of life he would still have. Fears was not particularly disturbed by the outcome. He'd seen men die before. But he was exhausted. It had been a long day for all of them, and so after delivering his news he went up to bed.

"We'll use it against Robinson to try to get a

confession out of him," Hughes said. "The man's partner dies, it might make him more apt to think about cutting a deal."

"If Robinson and McCay even did it," Lucy Blake said. "I'm not convinced."

"Nor am I," Hughes agreed.

The Palace Hotel was situated on the corner of Broadway and Bullard, so it was just down the road from many of the restaurants and saloons which seemed most prevalent on those two streets. The nearest saloon was the one where Hughes had seen the fight earlier. As such, they the noise coming from the saloons down the thoroughfare was little more than a low rumble of conversations with the occasional audible whoops as someone played a winning hand at a card table.

Hughes drew on his cigar and blew the smoke out toward a lantern hanging from a post on the fence separating the patio from the street.

"We're running out of time," Hughes said again. The nagging feeling had stuck with him through dinner. "Whoever did this is going to be gone soon, and once they're gone, we'll never find them."

"How can you be sure they're even still here?" Lucy asked.

While it was true that she headed up her own Pinkerton office in Albuquerque, Lucy did not have nearly the years of experience that Calvin Hughes had in investigating crimes. Her experience, prior to Albuquerque, was nothing more than filing papers and copying letters in the Denver office.

"It's just a hunch," Hughes said. "This was no small

149

job. Whoever did it, they went to lengths to confound the law. They tried to make it seem that Apache did it. Think about it. We've surmised that the deed was done, the safe was stolen, by the time the stagecoach topped the hill over the relay station. The four men who rode away – dressed as Apache – waited on that stagecoach. Right?"

"It certainly seems so," Lucy said. "We know for sure the safe was gone before the stagecoach arrived."

"So why not everyone leave together? Why wait for the stagecoach? Why risk being seen? They had the safe, they could have been gone. But they hung around – the four on horseback – to make certain they were seen."

"Yes," Lucy said. "That's absolutely how I read it."

"My guess is, they went to so much trouble to make it seem that this was an act committed by Apache because they planned to hang around the area, at least for a little while."

"But why?" Lucy asked.

"To take the stagecoach out," Hughes said. "It's the fastest way to get the farthest distance. But if there were six men, at least, they couldn't all board the stagecoach at the same time. Maybe they're leaving in pairs."

"Like Robinson and McCay."

"Yes. If they were involved," Hughes said.

"Or maybe they had to divvy up the loot," Lucy offered. "Someone took the safe to that abandoned prospecting camp where you found it. And four men rode to the Rio Grande. Maybe they doubled back and they all met here in Silver City."

Hughes nodded thoughtfully.

"That camp is north of here, by my best reckoning. It would have been easy for them to take the safe to that camp, bust it open to get the valuables inside, and then ride back here to meet the others."

Lucy frowned.

"So how do we find them?"

"If there were six men, they'd be looking at a thousand dollars apiece," Hughes said. "Plus the other valuables in the safe. That's a lot of money to come into. Can the resist the temptation to spread that money around some?"

Just then they heard a deadened cheer rise up from down the road. Both of them turned toward it, some hurrahing for another win on another poker table in one of the saloons.

"I wonder who is playing big stakes in Silver City who maybe never has before," Lucy said.

"I think I'm going to stroll down the road and visit some of Silver City's drinking and gambling establishments."

Lucy grinned and nodded.

"Would you be willing to accept a lady on your arm?"

"I'd be happy for the company."

* * *

If they'd been walking down the street in San Francisco or Chicago, St. Louis or New Orleans, Calvin Hughes would have felt like the king of the world.

Lucy Blake's hands, covered in black, lacy gloves and curled around the crook of his elbow, gave Hughes a feeling unfamiliar. He'd always enjoyed the company of women — too much, according to his boss James Hume. But something about having Lucy snuggled against his arm, feeling her breath on his cheek when she turned to whisper into his ear, made something in his chest catch. Though she was enchantingly pleasant, Lucy was also a distraction.

At least she wrapped herself against his left arm and kept his gun hand free.

The saloons in Silver City hardly conjured visions of San Francisco or New Orleans, and for Hughes, that's where the fantasy stopped.

They were dirty places, poorly lit, and they smelled of sweat, stale beer, and lamp oil.

For dinner, Lucy had changed into a satin gown with a shawl to keep her warm, and she was now thoroughly overdressed, drawing the attention of every man with eyes in his head. She was also the only woman Hughes saw in any of the saloons who did not seem to be working the upstairs rooms.

Nevertheless, they entered three different places as they came to them, in each one walking from the door to the back, and making a winding loop back to the door.

"We're looking for anyone who looks nervous," Hughes said to her from the corner of his mouth. "Anyone who either looks nervous at the tables, or nervous because we're in the place. By now, especially after Deputy Tucker shot McCay this morning, everyone in town is going to know that the woman with the eye patch is a Pinkerton detective."

But Hughes never got the impression that their presence made anyone nervous. Lusty stares turned their way – or, at least in Lucy's direction – but no furtive glances, no anxious stares, no uneasy fumbling of drink or cards. Hughes also did not see any evidence that anyone was playing at high roller. The antes he saw were all small.

As they stepped out of the third saloon, turning to continue down the street, Dan Tucker came trotting across the thoroughfare at them.

"Evening," Tucker said, touching a hand to his hat. "Understand that feller, McCay, died this afternoon."

"So we heard," Lucy Blake said.

"He shouldn't have tried to run," Tucker said, and then dismissed the topic entirely. "Look here, what are the two you thinking parading Miss Blake through these saloons?"

"We're just taking the air," Hughes said.

Tucker shook his head.

"That ain't smart, not here. This is a rough town, Hughes. This is not the sort of town where a lady in a fancy dress just saunters into a saloon. We've got prospectors here who haven't seen a proper woman in a decade."

Hughes chuckled, but Dan Tucker wasn't smiling.

"I'm serious. If there's something you need, maybe I can help you. Or maybe you should walk the saloons alone. But some of these characters wouldn't think twice of shoving a knife in your gut just to steal a kiss from Miss Blake."

Tucker's agitation was convincing.

"We're looking for anyone who might be showing fresh cash," Hughes said.

Tucker nodded.

"Someone who has just come into a lot of money," he said. He twisted his lips as he thought about it. "I haven't seen anything like that, and it's the sort of thing I would notice."

"You always patrol the saloons?" Hughes asked.

"I'm usually out in the evenings," Tucker said. "I make myself available for when there's trouble, and I'll walk through the saloons to see if I can find it starting. Best to head it off before it begins."

Hughes frowned and glanced at Lucy Blake. She gave a small shrug.

"We don't want to start any trouble," Lucy said. "If you think it's best, we can lay off walking through the saloons."

"I think it's best," Tucker said.

"But you'll keep an eye open for us?" she said. "Watch for anyone suddenly in some money?"

"I'll do that," Tucker said.

"What was that trouble at the saloon earlier this evening?" Hughes asked. "Two men fighting just at dusk."

Tucker grunted and shook his head.

"Damned Buffalo soldiers from Fort Bayard. Six of them mustered out a few days ago. They get to drinking, and it's never long before some Son of the South runs off at the mouth at them, and then I'm busting up a fight. I've had two of the six in my jail just since I got back from riding with

the posse. They're hell in an Indian fight. One of those boys
– Greaves – won the Medal of Honor for his part in an
Indian fight. And the truth is, every time I hear that the
Apache are off the reservation, I'm glad Fort Bayard is just
up the road. But when they come here on leave, or when
they hang around after retiring from the cavalry, it does
nothing but cause me aggravation. I'll be glad when this
bunch moves on."

- 15 -

"What is that?"

Hughes glanced at Lucy Blake, curled under the covers of his bed in the Palace Hotel. Her bare arm and shoulder showed, and she now pulled the blanket up to cover her shoulder. She wore only her eye patch. She'd come to be there after a remark about how chilly the night air had gotten. Hughes, who seldom missed an opportunity, suggested there might be a way to fight off the cold. To his surprise, Lucy didn't blush.

Afterward, Lucy dozed in his bed, but Calvin Hughes

could not sleep. The murders at the relay station, the theft of the Wells Fargo safe, and the sense that if he did not soon solve this case it would never be solved, they combined to trouble his mind. So he slid out of the covers and dressed himself in his shirt and trousers, and he lit a lamp and turned the wick down low and sat under the lamp with Roy Bennett's ledgers open on a table.

"One of the ledgers I found with the safe," Hughes said.

"Did you think of something?" Lucy asked, blinking her one eye against the light while she reached a hand out of the blanket to adjust her eye patch.

"Nothing specific. I just thought it was worth looking at again," Hughes said. "I'm running out of clues that might lead to something."

Lucy rolled now onto her back and sat up a little against the pillows, keeping the blanket up below her chin, less for modesty and more for warmth.

"If you get out of bed to read ledgers, does it not defeat the purpose of my seeking warmth against the night chill in your room?" Lucy asked with a grin.

"I suppose it does," Hughes conceded. "But I cannot shake the feeling that if we don't solve this soon, we will never solve it."

Lucy sighed and rolled out of bed, fetching her clothes from the clothes horse near the bed. She slid into her bloomers and undershirt and then wrapped her shawl around her shoulders. She sat on arm of the chair where Hughes was sitting and looked down at the ledger.

"What have you got here?" she said.

Hughes frowned.

"Not much of anything. This ledger indicates that a lot of people left various things at the relay station for safe keeping. A bag of gold dust," he said, pointing to a specific entry.

"Two hundred dollars in cash," Lucy said, pointing to another entry. "There was quite a bit more in that safe than just the mine's payroll."

"Yes," Hughes agreed. "Surely whoever took the safe knew the Gibbons & White Mining Company's payroll was there. That had to be the lure. But there were other valuables, certainly. Entries in this column, though, indicates that someone collected whatever they'd stored at the relay station. Here's a gold watch that was left by a man named Jasper. But this date here shows where he came and fetched it."

Hughes turned a page and both of them looked it over. He turned another page.

"Wait a minute," Lucy said. "What's this say?"

"A buckboard wagon," Hughes said. "I noticed that when I was at the relay station a couple of days ago. I looked around, and the wagon is no longer there. I'm confident that's the wagon they used to transport the safe to the mining camp, the one I found down in the ravine."

"Yes, but what's that name?"

"'L. Stellman,'" Hughes read.

"Yes, that's what I thought it said," Lucy said. "Could that be Lieutenant Stellman?"

"Certainly it could be," Hughes said, the tiniest hint of excitement in his voice.

"Why would a lieutenant stationed at Fort Bayard have need to store a wagon at the Wells Fargo relay station?"

Hughes shrugged.

"I couldn't say."

"A lieutenant would not travel to his post by wagon," Lucy said.

"I would not think so," Hughes agreed. "Train, then stagecoach to get to Fort Bayard. He probably came here from one of the military schools back east."

"Yes. He's young enough that we could assume this is his first post. So why does he have a wagon? Storing it for the army?"

"Again, I wouldn't think so," Hughes said. "Fort Bayard has plenty of places to park a wagon."

"We should ride out to Fort Bayard in the morning," Lucy said.

"Yes."

"And you should return to bed now."

Hughes grinned at her.

"Yes."

- 16 -

"I have duties to tend to," Lieutenant Stellman said irritably. "I'll give you a few minutes, but that's all."

"I understand you're leaving the cavalry," Hughes said.

Calvin Hughes and Lucy Blake had risen early. Lucy opted to go horseback rather than drive the wagon, so she wore a split riding skirt and took Hughes' spare horse. Hughes rode Sequoia. They left Albert Fears in Silver City to go and see if Josh Robinson was in any more of a mood to cooperate. They rode directly to Fort Bayard and found the lieutenant on the parade ground with a group of troopers. He sent the troopers off when Hughes said they'd like to talk to him about the murders at the relay station.

Lieutenant Stellman clenched his jaw.

"My folks have a place back in Missouri," Stellman said. "They raise horses. I've decided to return there and help them."

"Life in the cavalry wasn't what you thought it would be?" Hughes asked. He had an edge to his tone, and Lucy Blake frowned at the Wells Fargo man, wondering if he meant for that comment to sound as offensive as it did.

"I'm planning to help my folks," Stellman said.

"Tell me about the wagon you kept at the relay station," Hughes said.

Stellman seemed surprised, caught off guard by the question, and he squinted at Hughes, not answering for several moments. Then he said, "It's a wagon."

"Is it still there?" Hughes asked.

"I couldn't say," Stellman said. "I haven't looked to see."

"I find it strange, Lieutenant, that you would purchase a wagon here. Are you intending to drive yourself back to Missouri?"

Again, Stellman hesitated before answering.

"It's actually an army wagon," he said. "Until you mentioned it, I'd forgotten all about it."

"It wasn't that long ago that you took the wagon to the relay station," Hughes said. "Just a week before the robbery."

"What's this about?" Stellman snapped. "Why are the two of you not out chasing Apache?"

Hughes narrowed his eyes.

"When do you muster out, Lieutenant Stellman?"

"Tomorrow at dawn I am out of the army," Stellman said.

Hughes nodded thoughtfully.

"When did you learn that there were two months' worth of the Gibbons & White Mining Company's payroll in the safe at the relay station?" Hughes asked.

Stellman shook his head.

"I don't know anything about payroll at the relay station."

"It's convenient for you that the Santa Rita mine's payroll was double what it usually is, and that coincided with you mustering out of the army."

"What is this all about?" Stellman asked. "What are you implying?"

Hughes clenched his jaw and spoke through gritted teeth.

"I'm not implying anything, Lieutenant. I'm accusing. I think you found out about the payroll and cooked up a scheme to steal it."

The lieutenant's boyish face flushed red, and he could not hide that he was blushing. Red splotches broke out all over his cheeks and neck. Hughes had known men like that, men who could not hide a lie.

"You stole that payroll. You cooked up a scheme

and stole that payroll because you thought you could get out of New Mexico Territory before anyone figured out that it wasn't Apache."

"Absurd," he said. "I rode with the posse trying to catch the men who raided the relay station. You've leveled your accusation in the wrong place."

"And what better way to make certain you got away with it than to be both the man who stole the payroll and the man leading the charge to recover it?"

"Absurd," Stellman said again. "If you have some proof of this, then produce it, and I will defend myself. But you can't come here making accusations against me like this. Now get away from this fort before I have my troopers throw you in the guardhouse."

Hughes scoffed at the threat.

"Someone will be in the guardhouse," Hughes said. "You committed this crime while serving in the cavalry. I won't be surprised if it's a military trial for you."

Lucy Blake took a couple of steps back. A simple questioning of a man who she hadn't really yet thought of as a suspect had rapidly turned contentious, and Lucy wasn't even sure how it had happened.

"Absurd," Stellman said. "I led the posse. I didn't have anything to do with it, and I don't think I'm going to answer any more of your questions."

Stellman now took a couple of steps away, as if he was testing Hughes to see how he would respond if Stellman decided to just leave. Hughes did nothing, and so Stellman turned abruptly on his heel and began to walk away, leaving the two detectives standing in the fort's parade ground.

"I didn't expect that," Lucy said as they watched Stellman walk away.

"I don't think I did, either," Hughes said. "Something about his demeanor annoyed me. Anyway, he'll make a mistake now. Our job now is to make sure we catch him when he makes it."

Lucy stared aghast.

"You think he did it?"

"I know he did it," Hughes said, still watching Stellman walk away. "Did you see the way he blushed when he was caught?"

Lucy frowned.

"I don't know, Cal. That exchange got very heated. He might have turned red from anger, not from guilt."

Hughes grinned at her.

"That's a man who is about to make a mistake. Let's find a place where we can see it happen."

They took up their horses' reins and walked off the parade ground toward the small town built up near the fort. There were a couple of saloons, three small dry goods stores, a restaurant, an old cantina that might have been the first establishment at Fort Bayard, a church, and a dozen or so tradesmen with shops. Half the buildings in the town faced the fort, and the other half lined a street that ran south away from the fort.

Hughes and Lucy led their horses into a shady vacant lot where there was a tiny bit of grass and a trough full of water, and they tied the horses on long leads to a post. Then they walked along the boardwalk in front of the buildings facing the fort. At the end of the street was the saloon where Hughes had found Apache Tom, the half-breed scout. When they reached the saloon, Hughes glanced inside through the open door and saw the scout sitting at the bar. He had a bottle of liquor in front of him.

"Not in here," Hughes said as Lucy started to step inside. He quickly moved away from the door before the scout turned to see them. "Let's walk over to the cantina and get something to eat."

Though perplexed, Lucy did not argue.

She believed she could learn her craft from the Wells Fargo man. She knew he had a solid reputation back in California, and though she put a lot of stock in her own abilities, she was also aware of her own lack of experience.

The cantina had a small buffet on a table set up against a back wall. Spiced meat, flat bread, eggs and a pepper sauce. The buffet was free with a two-drink minimum, so Hughes ordered four whiskey drinks and each of them got a plate of food. Then they sat by the front window where they had a view of the fort.

"Tell me what's going on?" Lucy said.

Hughes grinned at her.

"The other morning, I witnessed Lieutenant Stellman and that army scout get into a heated argument," Hughes said. "It happened over there in that saloon. It wasn't an official argument, either. No army scout would officially argue with an officer, not if he wants to keep his job. My hunch is that the scout and the lieutenant are in this together. But they've got accomplices – the men who actually stole the safe and killed Roy Bennett and Clint Thacker."

Lucy moved the food around her plate with her

fork, but she did not eat it. Neither of them were hungry. Hughes' money went to rent a place to sit and watch the fort, not for a meal.

"Okay, so what mistake is he going to make? What are we watching for?"

Hughes pursed his lips and watched out the window a moment.

"A hunted animal, when it gets cornered, will do one of two things. It will either fight back or try to make a run."

"So we're watching for ..." Lucy paused and narrowed her eye at Hughes. "We're watching for the lieutenant to come across the street and start shooting at us through the window?"

Hughes shrugged.

"Maybe. Hopefully he doesn't know we're here. But maybe. Or maybe we're watching for him to go to the saloon. If I'm correct that the scout, Apache Tom, is his accomplice – or one of them – then he might go there."

Lucy blinked her eye.

"That's not running or fighting back," she said.

"That depends on what he says to Apache Tom."

***

The Wells Fargo agent and the Pinkerton detective kept their seats in the cantina through the greatest portion of an hour. Eventually, both of them began to pick at their food and sip at their drinks. The plates were empty when at last a man in an officer's uniform appeared on the parade ground, walking with a purpose toward the little town.

"Is that him?" Lucy asked.

"It could be," Hughes said. "Hard to tell from this distance."

But as he neared, it became clear to both of them that the man cutting out across the wide yard of the fort was in fact Lieutenant Stellman. Hughes and Lucy both leaned away from the window, hoping he would not notice them.

"If he looks like he's coming this way, duck down under the table," Hughes said. "But I don't think he's looking for us."

Stellman neared the road separating the fort from the town, and at that point his intention was clear. He cut a diagonal path that would lead him directly to the saloon. By the time he hit the boardwalk, he was out of sight. But the saloon sat on the far corner of the block, and there was nowhere else he could have gone.

"We should confirm he's gone in there," Hughes said.

"Without being seen?" Lucy asked.

"Preferably."

"Leave it to me," Lucy said.

She slid out of the booth before Hughes could stop her and dashed out the door of the cantina.

Hughes stood up and walked to the door of the cantina, his hand resting on his Schofield. He stood at the door waiting for any sign of a commotion. He propped the door of the cantina open with his foot, feeling the chilly morning air. He could just see down the boardwalk to the saloon where Lucy Blake had removed her hat and was peering into the window, much the same way Hughes had done when he'd witnessed the argument between Stellman and Apache Tom.

Suddenly, Lucy spun on her heels and started to dash back toward the cantina. She hopped out into the street so her heels wouldn't make noise across the boardwalk. Hughes kicked open the door just as Lucy neared the cantina. She sprang from the street, landing once on the boardwalk with a wooden thud, then she was through the door. Hughes pushed the door closed, and the two of them hurried back to their table by the window.

"Did they see you?" Hughes asked.

Lucy was breathing hard and laughing through the heavy breaths.

"No," she said. "But Stellman was turning to leave."

Just then, they saw Stellman emerge back out on the street, cutting back across toward the fort. He was not looking around as if he'd been aware of the spy who'd seen him talking to the army scout.

"They were talking to each other?" Hughes asked.

"Oh, yes," Lucy said. "Very animated. I would not say they were arguing, but definitely excited."

"You couldn't hear what they were saying?" Hughes asked, though he expected she could not because he'd not been able to hear anything of the conversation he witnessed, either.

"Nothing," Lucy said.

"It was a short conversation," Hughes noted.

"Just long enough to say the two detectives are onto them and something has to be done," Lucy said.

"If Apache Tom comes for us, it would probably be best not to kill him," Hughes said. "If we can help it. We'll need a confession out of him."

"You think that's it?" Lucy asked. "You think Stellman told Apache Tom to kill us?"

"I hope not," Hughes said. "They have other accomplices, and we need Stellman and Apache Tom to lead us to those accomplices. I hope Stellman told him to tell everyone involved to scatter."

Lucy grinned.

"Or meet up," she said.

"That would be nice," Hughes said. "But I doubt it."

"They have to meet up," Lucy said. "They have to divide up the money. Stellman and Apache Tom were riding with the posse immediately after the raid on the relay station. They haven't gotten their cut yet."

Hughes nodded.

"Maybe. If you're right, it would make everything very easy on us."

They did not have to wait five minutes before Apache Tom walked out of the saloon. He wasn't staggered drunk, but he had a bit of a sway in his step. He was walking out across the street toward the fort, but taking a different path than the one Stellman had followed. Stellman had been walking out across the parade ground toward the building that housed the officers' quarters. Apache Tom was walking a path that would lead him behind the barracks and toward the stables.

"What do you think?" Lucy asked.

"I think we'd better get our horses and be prepared to follow him," Hughes said.

- 17 -

Hughes walked to the edge of the block and then turned down to walk along the saloon. He stepped around the corner to the back of the building and stood there, trying to appear casual to anyone who might pass by while also trying to stay where he could see the fort stables but would not be seen Apache Tom when he came back out of the stable.

Hughes and Lucy Blake both reasoned that if Apache Tom had gone to the stables, he'd likely come out with a horse he intended to ride off someplace. So Hughes sent Lucy to the vacant lot to gather their horses and then take them the long way around to the back of the saloon in the hopes that Apache Tom would not see her. Hughes had visions of Apache Tom coming out of the stable on the back of a horse already at the gallop before Lucy ever turned up with their horses, and they'd lose their one best thread as quickly as they'd found it. But he needn't have worried. Lucy came at a trot, leading both of the horses.

"Cinch your saddle," Lucy said. "I didn't bother with it."

Hughes nodded as he took Sequoia's lead rope.

"Have you seen anything yet?"

"Not yet," Hughes said. "If he comes out the other side of the stable, I should still be able to see him ride away."

"What's your best guess?" Lucy asked. "Where's he going to go?"

"If he heads east, then my guess is that the accomplices are at the Santa Rita mine. That probably means McCay and Robinson were in it, too. If he cuts west, he's riding to Silver City and his accomplices will be there. If he goes north, then I'm going to bet they buried the payroll money up at that prospecting camp."

Lucy nodded as he spoke.

"That all sounds reasonable," she said. "You think we're about to break this open?"

"I do," Hughes said. "Unless we foul it up."

"Lose Apache Tom as he rides off?"

"Lose him, or he sees us and we end up trading shots with him and have to kill him," Hughes said. "I had a case once in California where I was going to follow the one good suspect I had, but he saw me following and laid in ambush for me. He shot at me, I shot at him, and before the day was over, I'd shot him three times. Killed him. Never did figure out who was in the stagecoach holdups with him."

It was idle talk, a memory of something that felt familiar to this. But Hughes also intended it to be instructive. He wanted Lucy to understand the possible consequences if they had to start shooting.

Several more minutes passed, and Hughes was beginning to wonder if the cavalry scout would emerge from the stable. But then Apache Tom appeared at the door of the stable, leading a saddled horse. Lucy had walked the two horses farther behind the saloon so they couldn't be seen.

"He's coming out, and he's got a horse saddled," Hughes said, stepping back so that he was just peering around the corner. He held his hat behind his back. "Mounting up. Heading west."

"Toward Silver City," Lucy said.

"Yep."

"Now we have to try to follow him without him knowing we're behind him."

"And how do we do that?" Lucy asked.

Hughes chuckled.

"Carefully."

He watched just long enough to be sure that Apache Tom was taking the road, and then he walked over to the big red roan. He adjusted his saddle and cinched the girth. Both of them stepped into their saddles and dragged reins toward the west to get their horses moving.

"Take it easy," Hughes said. "The key will be to spot him when we top ridges and when he's riding up hills in front of us. After he tops a hill, we can pick up the pace a little to be sure we don't get left too far behind."

This was open territory, broken only by the big juniper bushes that dotted the landscape. The juniper was big enough to hide behind, but any time Apache Tom was riding up an elevation, it wouldn't take much for him to turn in his saddle and see Hughes and Lucy behind him. There was nothing they could do about it, though. If they were going to follow the scout, they would have to risk exposing themselves.

So they did the best they could, keeping to the edges of the road where they could quickly pull their horses off into the juniper if they saw Apache Tom start to survey his backtrail. In the places where Apache Tom disappeared beyond a ridge ahead of them, Hughes and Lucy let the horses run, and when they topped the ridge, they always found they had closed the distance. They would stop then, and let Tom gain some distance on them. Then they'd continue the pursuit. When they were within sight of him, they always stayed at least four hundred yards behind him, close enough that they could see him but far enough back where if Apache Tom made a casual glance over his shoulder, he might not notice them.

After riding a couple of miles, they slipped down into a valley where the road seemed to tunnel through a canopy created by a forest of mesquite trees. Without the constant sun beating down on them, the morning air felt chilly again, and Lucy slipped into a coat she had tied to her saddle. But almost as soon as she had it on, they broke out into a wide pasture. Though he saw no cattle, Hughes assumed the pasture was part of a larger ranch.

They'd lost sight of the cavalry scout completely now, and Hughes was beginning to worry. Either Apache Tom had pushed hard up the road to outdistance them, or he'd taken some trail through the mesquite that they had missed.

"Should we double back?" Lucy asked.

"I'm not sure," Hughes said, twisting in his saddle to look around at their backtrail. He sighed heavily, indecision creeping over him. "If he rode off on some trail or just out through the pasture, we might never find him. I think we should just press ahead."

They were not far now from Silver City, just a couple of miles, and Hughes let Sequoia work into a good lope that took them out across what remained of the valley, and then they were climbing higher, up the last good slope before they came to Silver City. He hoped when they topped that ridge that they would see Apache Tom out in front of them somewhere, but at the top of the ridge all they saw were two men about a mile away riding toward them from the town.

As they come up level with the men, Hughes called to them.

"You didn't pass an Indian, did you?" Hughes asked.

"Didn't see nobody," one of the men answered.

Hughes frowned at Lucy.

"Looks like we lost him," Hughes said.

Lucy returned the frown.

"What now?" she asked.

"We're almost to Silver City," Hughes said. "Let's ride on into town and check in with Mr. Fears. Maybe I'll go back out to Fort Bayard this afternoon. If nothing else, we know where to find Lieutenant Stellman, at least until tomorrow morning."

***

The livery stable they'd been using since coming to Silver City sat at the south end of Bullard Street, and so they started in that direction with the horses when they arrived in the town. But as they neared the livery, Lucy Blake suddenly dragged her reins hard, pulling her horse in front of Sequoia and forcing Hughes to turn with her down an alleyway.

"What are you doing?" Hughes asked, but Lucy twisted in the saddle and shot him a look – her brows furrowed into a frown and her lips pursed tight. She gave the horse a touch with her heel to hurry it along, and Sequoia followed willingly.

"He's back there on the street," Lucy said.

"Apache Tom?"

"Yes. I think he's coming from the livery."

Lucy swung her leg over the horse and handed up her reins to Hughes.

"I'm going to follow him. Wait for me back at the hotel."

The Wells Fargo man started to argue, but Lucy ignored him and dashed out of the alley. Instinctively,

Hughes felt it was his place to follow Apache Tom, considering it might turn dangerous. But he stopped himself. It was no easier, now that they had shared a bed together, to think of Lucy Blake as a Pinkerton agent and not as a woman. The scar on her face and the eye patch served only as a reminder of how dangerous her job could be, dangerous that Calvin Hughes knew well enough and accepted for himself. But Lucy Blake also accepted those dangers for herself, and Hughes knew he could not now attempt to shield her from those dangerous – even if that violated his instincts.

Either Apache Tom knew a shortcut into Silver City or he'd run his horse at a gallop for the last bit of the ride over from Fort Bayard. Either way, he'd arrived long enough before Hughes and Lucy that he already had managed to leave his horse at the livery and was headed up the street.

Hughes held Sequoia where she was and also kept a tight grip on the spare horse's reins. He'd give Lucy a moment or two to begin trailing Apache Tom before he risked riding out of the alleyway and possibly exposing her. But his instinct was to quickly take the horses to the livery and then try to catch up to her and be there if Apache Tom spotted her.

As he sat in the alley, Hughes imagined a score of terrible consequences if Apache Tom saw Lucy, and he began to regret allowing their relationship to become something other than a friendly rivalry between competing investigators. Bedding her had been a mistake, he realized, because now his concern for her safety was overwhelming his focus on the tasks at hand.

After giving Apache Tom and Lucy Blake time to move down the street, Hughes rode out of the alley and down to the livery. After leaving the horses in the livery's corral, he walked back up Bullard Street a ways, looking for the cavalry scout or the Pinkerton agent, but he did not see either of them. He gave up looking for them and made his way back to the Palace Hotel to wait for Lucy's return.

Albert Fears was there, sitting on the patio outside.

"Where is Miss Blake?" Fears asked as Hughes stepped through the gate and onto the patio.

"Working," Hughes said.

"Any luck with the lieutenant?" Fears asked.

"Maybe," Hughes said. "I outright accused him of being involved in the theft and murders at the relay station."

Albert Fears chuckled at that and narrowed his eyes at Hughes.

"And how did he take it?"

"Angrily," Hughes said. "We observed him go and talk to the scout – Apache Tom. And then we followed the scout here to Silver City. Miss Blake is now trailing him down Bullard Street."

Fears had started to take a sip of the tea he was drinking, but he stopped with the glass halfway to his face.

"Alone?"

"Yes," Hughes said. "She told me to wait for her here."

Fears grunted and twisted his lips.

"I don't care for her being out there alone," he said.

"I don't either," Hughes agreed. "There wasn't much

stopping her, though."

Fears nodded, understanding. He'd not worked with Lucy Blake long, but he knew well enough her temperament.

"So what are we supposed to do?" Fears asked.

"Wait here," Hughes said. "She told me she would come and find us."

The waiting did not take long, but it was not Lucy Blake who turned up.

"Wells Fargo!" a deep, booming voice called out from down the road.

Hughes turned and saw Corporal Greaves riding in his direction.

"I wasn't sure I was going to find you," Greaves said.

"How did you find me?" Hughes asked.

"I checked at the liveries until I saw that red roan of yours," Greaves said. "When I found the horse, I asked where you were staying."

"I guess, more importantly, why did you find me?" Hughes asked.

Greaves had reached the small, brick fence at the patio now, and he pulled reins on his horse – a solid looking bay that was almost dark enough to be a black. Greaves made no move to get down out of the saddle. Like many men who spent their time on the back of a horse – wranglers and drifters, cowpunchers and cavalrymen – Greaves seemed more comfortable in the saddle than on his own two feet. He leaned forward some, resting his forearms across the saddle horn.

"I saw you this morning out at the fort," Greaves said. "Saw you talking to Lieutenant Stellman. Then I saw him go and fetch that drunken scout, Apache Tom, and Apache Tom rode off. Next thing I know, Lieutenant Stellman makes a request of the colonel to take his leave of us this afternoon instead of in the morning. He says to the colonel that he'd like to catch the stagecoach from Silver City in the morning, and if he's at the fort he's afraid he'll miss it."

"And what did the colonel say?" Hughes asked.

"Colonel don't care," Greaves said with a meaningful look. "Colonel shrugs and tells Stellman to do as he pleases, he's mustered out."

"So where is Stellman now?" Hughes asked.

"Last I saw him, he was packing his things and one of the troopers was going to drive him in a buggy here to Silver City this afternoon. I made an excuse to come to town for supplies, but I came to find you. My guess is that Lieutenant Stellman is halfway to Silver City by now."

Hughes glanced at Albert Fears.

"Why would you bother to come all the way here to tell me that?" Hughes asked.

"You wasn't talking to the lieutenant because he's a man with anything worth hearing," Greaves said. "I figure you've been adding things up in your head, and you've come up with two plus six equals eight."

Hughes shook his head.

"I'm not sure about eight," he said.

Greaves narrowed his eyes and cocked his head.

"Really?" he asked. "A couple weeks back we had six troopers muster out of the army. Today we had a lieutenant muster out, and a scout ride off on a cavalry horse that – unless I'm wrong – we'll never see again."

Hughes clenched his jaw.

"The six troopers that mustered out are the Apache who raided the relay station," Hughes said.

The accusation was a wild shot, but it had passed through Hughes' mind as a possibility.

Greaves shrugged his shoulders.

"I know some of those boys. I've served with them for a number of years. Two of them told me right before they left the fort that they're planning to buy cattle and start a ranch down near Roswell. You don't buy cattle on a cavalryman's wages, Mr. Wells Fargo."

"No, I reckon you don't," Hughes said. "What was their relationship with Stellman?"

"Same as mine," Greaves said. "They could not tolerate the man. But there in the last week or so, they was talking to him all the time. The six of them and Stellman, holed up together in private conversations. It struck me odd at the time. Like I said, some of those men are my friends, and I wanted to think the best of them. But when I saw you and Stellman talking today, and when he then asks the colonel to be turned loose to come here and catch the stagecoach – well, I know what I know."

"Why not catch the stagecoach at Fort Bayard?" Hughes asked. "It goes right past there."

"Exactly," Greaves said.

Hughes turned to Albert Fears.

"Why don't you go down to the jail and see if Deputy Tucker still has that man in a cell," Hughes suggested.

"Robinson?" Fears asked.

"No. The trooper who was fighting last night. Tucker arrested him and the man he was fighting with."

"Negro trooper?" Fears asked.

"Yes. He was fighting a white man outside the saloon just down the road there," Hughes said, pointing. "Tucker arrested both men."

"I'll go see," Albert Fears said, snatching his hat from the table and pushing it down tight on his head.

Hughes turned back to Greaves.

"Would you care for a drink, or a bite to eat?"

Greaves nodded.

"I could eat," he said, and he swung his leg over the horse's rump and dropped down from the saddle. His horse snatched a snack of its own from the bushes along the Palace Hotel's fence.

Hughes went inside and found the cook to bring them a meal. The woman fried up eggs and ham and brought two plates out to the patio. She did a double-take when she realized she was bringing a plate out to a Buffalo Soldier, but she made no comment about the presence of the soldier, nor about the fact that he was a black man. She set the plates down on the patio table and went back inside.

"Appreciate it," Greaves said, digging into the food as if he'd not eaten in some time. "Mess hall meals don't compare to this."

THE SANTA RITA PAYROLL

- 18 -

The boy wasn't more than about twelve years old, lanky and awkward with his new-found height. His clothes made a poor effort to keep up with him as he grew up and not out. His britches were cinched tight with a length of rope, and his white ankles showed under the cuffs of his pants. His coat would do to keep him warm right up to the wrists, but those were fully exposed and on a cold day he'd need to shove his hands inside the coat to keep the wrists warm. His face was dirty, but honest as he looked at the Wells Fargo man, the soldier, and the towering Pinkerton agent. But the one who really made the boy's eyes grow wide was the one who had a reputation locally – the deputy sheriff who was known to have gunned down men for anything from drunkenness to rock-throwing.

Albert Fears had returned several minutes before. Hughes and Greaves were just finishing their meals when Fears showed up, Dan Tucker tagging along.

"He let the soldier go this morning," Fears said. "But when I told him I thought we were getting close to breaking this case, he asked to come along."

"Pull up a chair, Deputy Tucker," Hughes invited. "You can join us in that long-honored tradition of lawmen everywhere: Waiting."

That had been maybe ten minutes ago, and in that time, Hughes laid out for Deputy Tucker all that he knew and suspected.

And then the boy turned up.

"I'm looking for Mr. Hughes, a guest at the Palace Hotel," the boy said.

"I'm Hughes."

"The lady with the eye patch sent me," the boy said. "She asked that you gather a couple of horses and meet her by the split cottonwood tree up by the corral at the north end of Bullard Street."

Hughes looked at Deputy Tucker.

"Big cottonwood, split by lightning a couple of years ago. Right at the north edge of town."

"Then I guess we'd better go," Hughes said.

The men split up.

Albert Fears went with Calvin Hughes down to the livery where Sequoia and Hughes' spare horse were being kept. Hughes got both his horses and saddled Sequoia for himself and the spare horse for Lucy. Albert Fears leased a big draught horse, one big enough to support his weight without trouble, and he saddled that one.

Dan Tucker hurried down to the corral out behind the jail where the sheriff's office kept a couple of horses.

Greaves, the only man present with a horse, walked his horse down Bullard Street in search of Lucy Blake. It was a risk, sending a man in uniform that the scout would know, but everyone agreed it was better to send someone as fast as possible in case Lucy ran into trouble.

But Greaves found no sign of Lucy Blake by the split cottonwood.

The old tree was a persistent thing. It had been split by lightning, blackening the skin of the tree in places and dropping a great big branch so that it looked as if the thing had been cut almost in half from the top to almost the bottom. The dropped branch still had a few brown leaves clinging to it, and the half still standing had a fair number of leaves. Though split like it was, and all the leaves now brown with winter and falling off into a circular pile, the tree still looked alive and robust. Greaves did not doubt that come spring, both halves would be rich in green leaves.

He reasoned it was possible she was hiding somewhere, avoiding detection by Apache Tom, and he did not spend much time trying to search her out. She wasn't expecting him and would not know that he was there to help her. So Greaves tied his horse to a hitching post in front of a dry goods store and took a seat on a bench out front of the store, and he waited there. He did his best to appear relaxed and indifferent while also looking around for Apache Tom or the recently mustered-out cavalry men. But he saw no one suspicious – not around the edge of town where a grove of tall pines marked the rise in elevation, not at the corral, not along the street. He saw nothing that seemed out of the way. Ordinary people going about ordinary business. A man and his son were talking to the liveryman about buying a riding horse for the boy, and the man argued about the price of every horse he was offered. Across the street a blacksmith was inside his shop, the door standing wide open, hammering away at something on his anvil. As he held it up in his tongs to put it back in the fire, Greaves thought it was taking the shape of a horseshoe. Down the road a half dozen women were standing on the front porch of a house – maybe a Bible study group or a sewing club. But he did not see Apache Tom. He did not see the woman with the eye patch. He did not see the men who had recently left the cavalry.

A couple of men who looked to be prospectors walked past, leading a mule a piece, heading north into the hills.

And then, coming up the road, Greaves saw Deputy Dan Tucker. He was riding a white gelding. Like Greaves, Tucker was scanning the street, looking for any sign of trouble or of the woman with the eye patch. His eyes locked with Greaves, but Tucker gave no recognition. Instead, he slid off his horse and tied it to the same post where Greaves had tied his horse. Tucker then walked into the store, not ever acknowledging Corporal Greaves.

Greaves noted that Tucker's horse was laden with gear – a canteen strapped to the saddle horn, a Winchester rifle in a sheath, saddlebags behind the saddle, a blanket rolled up and strapped to the back of the saddle. Dan

Tucker had come ready for whatever might happen. All Greaves had on his horse was a half-full canteen.

Several more minutes passed, and then Greaves saw Hughes and Albert Fears. Hughes was riding the red roan. Fears was up on a big draught horse, looking enormous. Hughes held the lead of another horse.

The two men dismounted in front of the store, and Hughes tied his two horses to a second post while Fears lashed his to the same post where Greaves and Tucker had tied their horses.

"The deputy went inside," Greaves said.

"Any sign of Miss Blake?"

"I've not seen her," Greaves said. "But if she's in hiding somewhere, watching, I doubt she'd show herself to me. I figured she would make herself known when you got here."

Hughes and Albert Fears stood out in the street where Lucy would be able to easily see them, but she did not immediately appear. Then Dan Tucker came out of the store.

"I know the owner here," he said. "I asked if he'd seen a woman with an eye patch, and she was here earlier. He didn't see where she went. He also said those Buffalo Soldiers from the fort have been hanging around here most of the last couple of weeks. He thinks they've been camping up in the pine forest north of town. Said he sees them just about every morning."

Hughes slid his Winchester rifle from its scabbard. He lowered the lever about half way to be sure there was a round chambered, and then he carried it lazily in his crossed arms.

"I'm going to walk up a ways and have a look," he said. "You fellows wait here for me, and listen for shooting."

***

Hughes took no time in finding the campsite. About half a mile up the road, not even particularly deep into the trees, Hughes saw from the road a clearing and a worn path leading over to it. Empty bean cans still moist with sauce were tossed off the side of the campsite. Hughes put his hand over the gray ash of the campfire. It was a sizable fire pit, suggesting it had been put to use over some time. As he pressed his palm down to the ashes, they felt cold, but Hughes brushed some off the top layer and found warm coals. The fire had burned that morning.

Hughes picked around the campsite a moment more. At the edge of the clearing he found prints, cropped grass, and other evidence that suggested a number of horses had been tied there for some time. Easily a half dozen. He followed those tracks back out the same path he'd taken in, and they clearly turned north on the road. But there he lost the tracks as they mingled with the tracks of the horses and mules that prospectors and others took up into the mountains.

But he'd seen enough to satisfy himself. He started to head back to the store to collect the others, convinced that the six cavalrymen had headed north, but then he saw one more indention in the ground that caught his attention. A track made by a narrow boot heel. Hughes studied it for a moment. It seemed fresh as it stood out there in the roadway among a hundred other tracks.

Now he jogged back down the road, emerging from the trees and waving to the others to mount up.

"I found a campsite up there, and tracks headed north," Hughes reported as he cinched the saddle on Sequoia. "I think they rode north. I think I know where they were going. And I think Lucy is following them."

"Following them?" Albert Fears asked. "On foot?"

"I think so," Hughes said.

The men all stepped into their saddles. Fears' rented horse balked at the notion and spun a circle as Fears tried to get his foot into the stirrup. Hughes, already on Sequoia's back, stepped the big roan over beside the draught horse to bar it from spinning, and Fears finally got purchase with his foot and swung himself over and into the saddle. Now the men started up the road at a trot.

"You don't have to be a part of this," Hughes said to Greaves.

The man shrugged his shoulders.

"I've come this far," he said. "Might as well see it out."

Hughes anticipated that it would not take them long to ride up on Lucy Blake. She'd still been in town when she sent him the message to come to the split cottonwood, and that had not been more than three quarters of an hour before the men set off up the road. He figured she was maybe two miles up the road. But even when they'd gone roughly three miles, there had been no sign of her. They trotted in short distances, but then slowed to a walk frequently, trying to make sure they did not miss some sign that the riders they were following – and the Pinkerton woman – had left the trail.

"Where do you think they're going?" Deputy Tucker asked when they'd made at least three miles.

"A couple of days ago I tracked a wagon from the Santa Rita relay station up to an abandoned prospector's camp," Hughes said. "That had to be somewhere north of Silver City, but I came at it from the southeast, so I'm not sure where exactly. I found the safe there, broken open, and a wagon tossed down a ravine into the creek."

Tucker thought about all the camps he knew north of town.

"How big was the camp?" he asked.

"A few cabins. It was a decent sized camp, for sure. Probably housed fifteen or twenty men, would be my guess."

Tucker nodded.

"That's going to be the camp up on Bear Creek," he said. "Been empty more than a year now when the claim panned out. The fellows that had it made a decent sum."

"Do you know the way?" Hughes asked.

"It's up this road, probably another six miles or so, and then a trail cuts off to the camp itself."

"Something must have happened to Miss Blake," Albert Fears said. "No way did she follow them this far without us catching up to her."

Hughes agreed. He hadn't wanted to say it aloud, though. Saying a thing always made it more real.

"If you know the way, Tucker, then take the lead," Hughes said. "Let's get there."

Dan Tucker nodded his head and without a word urged his horse forward to the lead of the pack, and in a moment, they were at a lope, driving deeper into the lodgepole pine forest, up the road that had carried hundreds of prospectors and their dreams.

They passed through a small town, just a couple of stores, a smithy, and a saloon. The place was all but deserted – the men around here would be hard at work, freezing their hands and feet in cold streams or tunneling deep holes in the ground.

As they went, they came across no sign of Lucy Blake.

Hughes imagined that she'd followed the scout through town to the camp where the half-dozen Buffalo Soldiers had been living these past several days. They must have seen her and taken her with them. At least, that's what he hoped. Maybe she was in a ditch somewhere, shot dead.

The scout, though, must have left his horse at the livery, and Hughes reasoned that he left it there for Stellman to take once he arrived in Silver City. Maybe the Buffalo Soldiers had a spare horse for him.

With the tall pines surrounding them, and the hills climbing higher, it seemed like they'd entered a different world at the boundary of the town. The forest was quiet, except for their own horses, the rattle of their gear, and the songs of the birds in the surrounding trees.

At last, Dan Tucker reined up and spun his horse around to face the others.

"We should go on foot from here," he said. "The trail to the camp is just up ahead."

- 19 -

Lucy Blake cursed her lack of caution.

She'd followed Apache Tom all the way out to the edge of Silver City where he'd walked out across a cleared area beyond a livery stable and following the road north into a pine forest. Lucy stood for a while behind a split cottonwood tree, watching for the man to emerge from the woods, but he did not come out immediately. And that was when she called over the boy who was idling at the nearby store, putting a coin in his hand and sending him to find Calvin Hughes at the Palace Hotel.

Then Lucy set out on her own, following the road into the forest.

She didn't get particularly far into the woods when Apache Tom stepped out from behind a bush. He held a long-bladed knife in his hand and a nasty smile on his face.

"That way," Tom said, nodding at a trail running down into the woods.

Lucy leaned back heavily, driving the heel of her boot into the ground – it was all she could do.

Apache Tom hurried her down the trail where they encountered a half-dozen men, all of them black men and some of them wearing pieces of cavalry uniforms. Tom roughly pushed Lucy to the ground and then had a quick conversation with the men.

"Stellman wants us to meet at the camp this evening," Tom said. "Says the law is asking questions and we need to all get out of here now. We're dividing the money tonight."

The cavalrymen broke camp in a hurry. They were efficient in the work – men practiced at moving quickly. They had no tents, just blankets they used for bedding. The men had a dozen horses tied below their camp. They tied makeshift reins from lengths of rope so that Apache Tom and Lucy Blake could each ride a horse, and then they set out. Lucy figured they weren't fifteen minutes getting out of the camp and starting up the road.

Lucy's message to Calvin Hughes was to fetch horses. She knew that there was no way he would arrive before they left the camp, and she was right. They went north, higher into the mountains and deeper into the forest. They rode through a small town that looked almost entirely abandoned. They rode at a quick pace. The men knew where they were headed, and they did not linger nor try to spare their horses.

Lucy figured they were probably a dozen miles or more north of Silver City when they finally left the main road. They cut out through the forest now, no clear path, riding between pines and spread out to avoid leaving noticeable tracks in the pine straw covering the ground.

The topped a rise and followed the ridge some way through the forest, all the while Lucy could hear a creek dropping down tiny falls and flowing over boulders, a mountain stream whose noise likely belied how small in volume it actually was. They followed the ridge a short distance, and then came upon a clear path where the riders converged. Now, down below the ridge, Lucy could see the stream as it plunged over a rocky cliff and dropped ten feet or so. As she suspected, the stream wasn't very large, but it made a tremendous cacophony in the deep, narrow ravine below the trail.

As they continued on, with the stream down below them, Lucy saw a wagon in the ravine. It looked as if it had been pushed over the edge. She was certain now that they were going to the prospecting camp that Hughes had described to her. Here, one of the men called to the others to hold up, and the cavalry scout reached out and took hold to Lucy's reins to keep her horse in place. One of the men rode forward a ways, and Lucy lost him in the forest. He was gone about ten minutes, and the others all just sat mounted on their horses, waiting on the trail. They talked some, but only among themselves and just idle talk.

But then one of the men turned to the scout and said, "What are you going to do with that woman?"

"Stellman can figure that out," the scout said. "Probably shoot her."

A benefit to being a woman, Lucy still had strapped to her thigh a Remington Model 95, a small two-shot over-under derringer pistol. The men never searched her, as they likely would have searched a man. Even thieves often had honor when it came to how they treated a woman, as Lucy well knew. When she worked in the Pinkerton office in Denver, she'd read dozens of reports of stagecoach robberies where the women were left with all their valuables, unmolested by the thieves.

Lucy remained stolid, even in the face of the threat.

The soldier who'd ridden forward returned to a spot where he could see the others and called up to them.

"It's clear down there!"

The others then started forward. Apache Tom gave a jerk to Lucy's reins to get her horse started.

As they rounded a bend and the path dropped down closer to the stream, Lucy could see several buildings. Rough-built log cabins. She spotted the broken safe. She had no question now that this was the place where Hughes had found the safe and the ledger with Stellman's name.

The place was clearly abandoned, as Hughes had described it.

Now the men dismounted. Lucy swung herself down out of her saddle, and Apache Tom took her roughly by the arm, dragging her toward one of the log cabins. She was not sure what he intended, but she decided if he meant to harm her, she would shoot and kill him and then deal with the others as she could.

He dragged her forcefully, roughly, up the steps of the log cabin, and when they reached the door, Apache Tom stopped and looked around inside.

There were pieces of broken and discarded furniture – tables and chairs and bunks, straw mattresses decaying. The place smelled of mold and dirt.

"You stay in here," Tom said, pushing Lucy through the door so that she stumbled and fell over. "If you come out, we will shoot you."

From the doorway of her makeshift jail, Lucy could see the men as they went about stringing a line and tying their horses, removing their saddles. All of the men were armed with rifles and six-shooters, and Lucy watched them as two of the men posted up as guards at the trail head. One of the men went down to the creek with his rifle, and Lucy lost sight of him as he burrowed into some brush. She figured he was watching the creek to make certain no one approached the campsite from that direction.

Apache Tom and the remaining three men gathered near the safe. As she watched, Lucy saw one of them dash over to another of the log cabins, and when he returned, he had a shovel with him. The man with the shovel went over to a spot under a couple of pine trees and kicked away the pine straw there, and then he began to dig. The earth seemed to be loose, and he had no trouble getting down a couple of feet. And then he tossed aside the shovel and got down on his knees, and Lucy watched as he plucked a couple of leather bags from the hole.

That was it, she thought, the Santa Rita payroll.

- 20 -

"There's no evidence of tracks on this trail," Dan Tucker admitted.

Tucker had swung down out of the saddle and was squatting down on one knee, looking hard at the ground.

"Seven or eight riders should have left some marks on the ground," Corporal Greaves said.

Calvin Hughes sat up tall on Sequoia's back and looked around at the surrounding forest, as if he hoped to see some evidence that the men they were trailing had come this way.

"Maybe they rode through the forest to avoid leaving a trail we could follow," Hughes said.

"Could be," Tucker said. "We've only got a couple of hours before it starts getting dark. It seems our best option is to ride down to the camp and check it out, since we're here anyway."

Hughes nodded.

"We'll have to go easy," Hughes said. "We can't do anything that might jeopardize Miss Blake."

"If she's still alive," Tucker said.

So despite the lack of tracks, the four men rode on along the trail. They went slowly, watching carefully through the woods for anyone who might be keeping a lookout. They did not go far before they came to another trail that came in from the southeast.

"This is the trail I took when I came up here a few days ago," Hughes said. "This trail leads down to the east of the Santa Rita mine and the relay station, and this is the one they took when they brought the safe up."

A short distance later, they dropped over a ridge, and Dan Tucker – still leading the party – dragged his reins to stop his horse.

"Look there," he said, pointing to the ground. "Those are fresh tracks."

Hughes peered down at the dirt, and indeed he saw fresh tracks in the ground. Several riders had come through here.

"They must've rid through the forest instead of turning off at the trail," Tucker said. "Did it so there wouldn't be tracks at the trail head."

Hughes glanced at Fears who glanced back at him and grinned. Tucker seemed pleased with himself to have guessed at what Calvin Hughes had already deduced.

"Might be best to stop here," Hughes said. "That camp ain't far along this path, now. I'm going to see if I can't follow this ridge and get up over it without them seeing me."

"Reconnoiter the camp," Corporal Greaves said. "Be smart to have a look before we go down there half-cocked. We don't want to dash in there if they're holding that woman hostage. They'd be liable to shoot her."

"We've got one more man who still hasn't turned up," Hughes said. "Might be smart for y'all to take these horses up beyond that ridge and watch this trail for Lieutenant Stellman."

Hughes dismounted and slid his Winchester from its scabbard.

Dan Tucker swung himself down out of his saddle and took Hughes by the arm before the Wells Fargo man was able to start away.

"Listen to me," he said. "Dark is coming soon. Those are Indian fighters down there in that camp. I don't intend to get caught here after dark trying to defend ourselves against a bunch of Indian fighters. You understand?"

Hughes bit his lip and nodded a short, curt nod.

"If you want to ride on back to Silver City, Deputy Tucker, all I ask is that you do your best to avoid Stellman, assuming he's somewhere on the road behind us."

Dan Tucker shook his head, a disgusted look on his face.

"I ain't talking about tucking tail and running," Tucker said. "I'm saying that as soon as the lieutenant rides into the camp, I'm following him in and arresting these men."

Hughes shook his head.

"We don't have enough evidence to make a case," Hughes said.

Tucker grinned at him.

"Those are Indian fighters, Mr. Hughes," Tucker said. "There won't be a trial. It'll be a shootout, and I'm telling you so that you're ready. When the lieutenant rides in, I'm following him. When I announce myself, those cavalrymen are going to go to shooting, and I'm going to shoot back. When I go to shooting, there won't be a trial. None of them are going to spend so much as a night in my jail."

"We need to make sure they have the money or something that proves they did it," Hughes said.

"Hell, we all know they did it. Now go and see if you can rescue your girl – if she's even there."

Hughes did not continue the argument – there was not time to argue.

While the others led the horses into the forest and over the ridge, Hughes took a different path, following the hill that circled around over the abandoned mining camp. The hill was steep in places, and he had to be careful about where he placed his feet to avoid slipping down and making a commotion that might alert anyone watching below.

He followed the hill around a route that kept him about ten yards above the trail, but as the trail began to descend toward the stream, Hughes found himself higher and higher above the trail.

The pines and undergrowth along the hillside were not particularly dense, but they combined to make visibility almost impossible. Hughes found himself up over the clearing where the mining camp was, but through the canopy of the pines and the brush on the hillside, he wasn't able to catch more than a glimpse of the cabins below him. So he continued to work his way along the hill, moving slowly and cautiously.

Hughes was aware, too, that time was against him. The shadows began to grow deeper as the sun came close to touching the ridge overlooking the western bank of the stream.

Finally, using a stout pine tree to steady himself, Hughes found himself in a position where he could peer around the edge of the tree and see the cabins below.

Almost directly below him, about sixty or seventy feet down the slope, Hughes saw a dozen horses tied to a line. Several saddles were set not far from the horses.

He could see four men – three black men, one of them wearing a cavalryman's britches, and Apache Tom. They were huddled together, near the safe. One of the black men was actually leaning against the safe.

There were supposed to be six of the soldiers, plus Apache Tom. The three missing men, Hughes reasoned, must be keeping a lookout somewhere. He scanned the rest of the camp but saw no evidence of the three missing soldiers, nor did he see any sign that Lucy Blake was with them. The thought occurred to him again that they might have cut her throat and dropped her into a ditch back at the Silver City camp.

But before Hughes and the others could storm in there, he desperately needed to know where the other men were, and he needed to satisfy himself that Lucy Blake was not actually with them.

He needed a closer look.

Hughes worked his way along the hill, back the way he'd come. When he reached a spot where the drop to the cabins was not quite so steep, he started down the hill, his feet turned against the slope of the hills so that he was actually walking down it sideways. In places he had to grab saplings and roots to steady himself.

As he descended and got below the canopy of the pines, the campsite came into fuller view. The men gathered down around the safe were all facing away from him, so he did not worry overmuch that he would be seen, but he still moved cautiously, trying to keep behind the undergrowth. The roof of one of the cabins was soon directly in front of him, almost close enough that he could leap out and land on it, and now he was entirely protected from being seen by the men near the safe. He moved a bit farther down, and then was just feet away from where the ground leveled out into a narrow flat between the hillside and the creek. Especially at the time it was occupied, it had been the perfect place to build a little camp, secluded and well hidden from the Apache raiders who sometimes harassed prospectors in the hills around Silver City.

Hughes jumped the last couple of feet, landing with one hand against the back of the cabin.

He pulled his hat from his head and peered around the edge of the cabin. Only the man leaning against the Wells Fargo safe was visible to him, and Hughes could see that the man was armed with both a rifle and a gun on his hip.

Clearly the men were waiting for Stellman. He did not think he had evidence enough to convict them at trial. All he could prove now was that these men had come into the camp where the safe had been abandoned by whoever stole it. That wasn't proof of much. But Hughes also knew that evidence sufficient for an arrest was not the same as evidence sufficient for certainty. He was certain now that these men were the ones who attacked and killed Roy Bennett and Clint Thacker and stole the Santa Rita payroll.

But Hughes knew that the evidence he had would never satisfy James Hume, even if he could somehow make a case to a jury. James Hume demanded from his agents a professionalism beyond what most sheriffs or prosecutors or judges required in a rough territory where cases were most often settled not by evidence but by how many friends a defendant had on his jury.

Certainly, James Hume required more evidence than what was needed to satisfy Dangerous Dan Tucker who already announced his desire to ride in and open fire.

What he needed was the money, or at least the money sacks marked Gibbons & White.

Hughes crossed along the back of the cabin to the other side, trying to get in a position where he could see the others. He snuck along the outside wall of the cabin, inching slowly toward the front where he might be able to get a look around to the front of the cabin. He focused on his footfalls, making certain he would not step in a hole and stumble or kick a discarded can or step down on a twig and break it.

Focused on the men in front of him and where he placed his steps, Hughes did not notice the men up the trail, the two men who'd been posted as lookouts to watch the trail. They were both of them hidden among the underbrush. But one of the two men turned back to look at the camp, and he saw Hughes sneaking along the side of the cabin. He called to his partner, and in a moment, both men were looking down the sights of their rifles.

- 21 -

The first shot broke loose splinters from a log in the wall just behind where Hughes stood. The second shot struck the dirt a few feet away. The burst of gunfire caught Hughes out in the open, exposed to both men shooting. The third shot struck the cabin wall behind him again, and it was that third shot that forced him forward, toward the front of the cabin, toward the men gathered in front of the cabin near the broken safe.

The Wells Fargo man did not know where the two shooters were, but he knew what to expect when he came around the corner of the cabin.

At least, he thought he knew what to expect.

Another shot, and then another sounded. Where the rounds hit, Hughes couldn't say. He dashed forward, prepared to face Apache Tom and the three cavalrymen. He rounded the corner of the cabin, his Winchester rifle up, the butt pressed into his shoulder. He was looking for a gun in a hand. It was seconds since the first shot sounded. Maybe none of them had reached for an iron, but the first man who cleared leather would be the most dangerous, the first one he would have to put down. So Hughes came around the corner, his eyes scanning the spot where he expected to find the cluster of men, searching for one who had already drawn his sidearm.

But what he found was not four men ready to confront an unknown threat. The four men were all running for the cover of the tree line between the clearing where the cabins set and the bank of the creek.

It stopped him short to see the men dashing for cover.

Another shot rang out from the lookouts posted to his left, and the bullet hit the log cabin with a thud as the lead buried itself inside the soft wood of the pine.

Hughes spun now, searching for the men shooting at him.

A small puff of white smoke led him to one of the shooters, hidden in a tangle of brush. Hughes squeezed the trigger on the Winchester. The long rifle barked and sent a shot spinning into the underbrush, but whether it took effect he had no idea.

And that's when he heard a shot from behind him, so close that he was sure he must have been hit. But when he spun to face the shooter, he saw Lucy Blake in the doorway of the cabin, smoke drifting from the small pistol in her hand.

"You'll be safer in here," Lucy suggested.

Hughes took three great strides and all but flung himself through the open doorway just as the four men who'd retreated into the tree line opened fire on the front of the cabin. Hughes and Lucy both cowered behind the walls of the cabin, away from the open doorway, as the cavalrymen and the scout fired two quick volleys into the cabin front.

"Glad to see you," Lucy said when the second volley subsided.

"I'm glad to see you," Hughes said, looking around the interior of the cabin. "We weren't sure if you were a body in a ditch somewhere or if you'd been taken hostage."

"Hostage," Lucy said. "But they left me with a gun."

Hughes leaned the Winchester against the wall and then scrambled across the floor of the cabin to an overturned table. He flipped it onto its side and then pushed it up against the door. It blocked the open doorway about halfway up, giving him a breastwork to fire from behind. As soon as he slid it into place, the men in the trees opened up with another volley.

"What's our situation?" Lucy said.

"We're pinned down," Hughes said.

Lucy laughed, and Hughes detected a touch of nervousness.

"Al Fears is out there, and he's got Corporal Greaves and Deputy Tucker with him," Hughes said.

Just then, the two inside the cabin heard a smattering of gunfire off to the east, coming from the trail that led down into the camp.

"That's them," Hughes said confidently.

From what Hughes could discern, the shooting came from hill above the camp and seemed to be directed toward the two men on lookout who had exposed themselves with their early shots. The men in the tree line were now spreading out, finding better positions. Hughes watched them over the lip of the table he had pushed against the doorway as he hunkered down low behind the table. And that's when he saw what had garnered the attention of the men who had been huddled around the safe, realizing for the first time what it was sitting there. Two substantial leather sacks, both with handles.

"Is that the payroll?" Hughes asked.

"They were counting it when the shooting started, planning to divide it up," Lucy said. "When we arrived here, they put me in this cabin and one of them took a shovel, walked directly to the spot, and dug up the money."

For several moments, the gunfire had subsided. But then there was another burst of activity, shots fired from up on the hill and return shots from the two men at the edge of the camp. Those shots seemed to spur the men down along the tree line, who had all taken up new positions and now sent several shots at the cabin from behind the cover of pine trees.

Hughes jerked himself back behind the thick walls of the log cabin as bullets punched into the table and sent splinters out the back.

"The payroll sitting out there, that's the evidence

that damns this group," Hughes said.

"Yes, certainly."

"Stellman still is not here," Hughes said.

"He'd be a fool to show up with all this shooting going on," Lucy said.

As the volley from the men behind the pine trees subsided, Hughes chanced a look over around the door frame. He was on his knees so that he could stay low behind the table, and he'd set his hat on the cabin floor.

He could clearly see one of the men. It was one of the soldiers, and though he'd taken a position behind a tree, his leg was entirely exposed as he squatted low.

Hughes took up his Winchester and in a quick movement swung the gun around the door frame. He took a fast aim at the place where he'd seen the exposed leg and fired a shot. The boom in the confined space of the cabin was deafening, and Hughes pulled back to the cover behind the cabin wall, unsure what damage he'd inflicted.

He chanced a glance around the corner of the door frame. The exposed leg had been tucked in. The man was still hunkered down behind the pine tree, apparently unhurt.

"We're in a bad spot," Hughes said.

As if on cue, another volley erupted from the men down along the tree line.

***

The bags of money sat out in the yard, almost equal distance between the two private detectives inside the cabin and the four thieves posted behind pine trees along the wood line.

Each time Calvin Hughes chanced a look at his adversaries, those two bags of money containing the Santa Rita payroll seemed to glow like beacons in the dying light of the day.

"It's getting dark fast," Lucy commented, as if reading Hughes' thoughts.

"It is. And once it gets dark, we're in a bad spot."

It had been a full minute, maybe more, since they'd heard any shooting from the hillside. Pinned down by gunmen with superior numbers, a full minute for those two inside the cabin seemed interminable. Not knowing what was happening with Albert Fears and the other two made it worse. They would not withdraw and abandon the two detectives inside the cabin, but whether or not they could get near enough and act soon enough seemed an open question.

"We have to figure it's going to be on us to get ourselves out of this," Hughes said.

"I'm open to suggestions," Lucy said.

"How many more shots do you have in that little gun?" Hughes asked.

"It's just two shots, and I've spent them both."

She'd fired both shots to scatter the men counting the money as Hughes was coming around the side of the cabin.

"No spare rounds?" Hughes asked.

"I am afraid not," Lucy said.

Hughes slid his Schofield six-shooter from its holster and opened the top break. He knew the gun's six chambers were loaded, but he checked from force of habit.

"You take this," Hughes said, handing over the six-shooter. "It's not the right tool for this situation, but it's better than an empty derringer."

"Do you have a plan?" Lucy asked.

"No. But somehow we need to even up the numbers as best we can," Hughes said. "I count the four of them and two at the front. But that's just six, and with Apache Tom they should be seven."

"They are seven," Lucy said. "One of them walked down into the brush by the river, I guess to be a lookout over in that direction."

"He could have moved by now," Hughes said. "So there are seven of them, and five of us."

"I count two of us," Lucy said.

"I'm including Mr. Fears and his friends on the hillside."

"Oh. Of course."

Hughes glanced around the cabin again, looking to see if they had some advantage he had overlooked.

"Come with me. Stay in the shadows."

Together, the two of them moved through the dark cabin toward the back wall, staying away from the open doorway. The light outside was growing so dim that inside the cabin it was almost pitch black. The cabin had no windows, and the only light was that which came through the door. At the back of the cabin, Hughes and Lucy could move freely without worry that they would become targets. The men at the pine trees would never see them moving around inside the darkened cabin.

Now Hughes moved carefully, peering out through the open door, changing his position, trying to get himself in a vantage where he might have a shot at one of the men outside. Here, in the shadows at the back of the cabin, Hughes had time to take find his shot and take aim.

At last he found an exposed shoulder. The man was wearing a red shirt, and his shoulder, as he held his rifle pointed toward the cabin, stuck out from the edge of the pine tree, the red shirt glowing like the bullseye of a target.

Easy breathing. The tiniest of pressure on the trigger. Exhale. Squeeze.

No shots had been fired, either on the hillside or down in the camp, and the big boom of the Winchester reverberating inside the cabin must have come like a clap of thunder from a cloudless sky.

That's what Hughes wanted – to rattle the men. Just when they were lulled into comfort, believing they found themselves in a standoff.

Better, the bullet smashed into the exposed shoulder, and through the doorway, Hughes saw the man recoil and flop onto the ground, screaming in agony. The bullet must have shattered a bone for all the wailing the man was doing.

Hughes and Lucy both dropped to the floor as the others behind the pine trees shook from the stupor and fired several shots into the cabin. All the while, though, even over the repeated gunfire, the man let loose screams of agony.

"That's what we needed," Hughes said to Lucy. "A couple more like that, and we might get out of this thing alive."

When the volley from outside the cabin came to an end, Hughes resumed his spot, standing at the back of the cabin and looking down the sights of the Winchester. He watched as one of the men dashed over to his injured comrade, applying first aid.

For every man you wound, you take two out of the fight. Hughes thought that was a quote he'd read from a general in the War Between the States. Maybe it was something James Hume had said to him. Either way, the axiom held true today.

"He's hit bad," the impromptu medic called to the others, loud enough that Hughes could hear him inside the cabin.

But more importantly than what he could hear, Hughes could see the man, crouched over his wounded comrade. The man was hunched down on all fours, pressing a bandanna against the injured man's shoulder. But he'd left his rear up in the air, and his thigh was entirely exposed. Now Hughes intended to make the axiom more true. He breathed out and squeezed the trigger.

"Ah! Lord have mercy!" the man shouted, and he rolled onto his back, clutching at the hole in the side of his leg.

Unless he'd struck an artery, Hughes did not think the wound was mortal. From the way the man was moving the leg as he roiled on the ground, Hughes thought it was likely a through-and-through wound. But that was two men effectively removed from the fight.

Now there was a renewed explosion of shots up on the hillside. Albert Fears, the deputy, and the corporal were playing hell with those two men on lookout. The shooting was incessant, but it wasn't coming in volleys. It was staggered, and maybe not precise, but the men on the hill clearly had their target picked out and had coordinated their attack against him. And then a yelp.

Lucy slid to the side of the cabin and made her way along the wall, watching out the door to try to position herself to see what was happening.

"Oh, my!" she exclaimed suddenly.

Hughes stepped over to where she was and looked out the door. One of the men in the brush who'd been at the edge of the camp on lookout had broken free of his cover and was running back into the camp. But he held himself in an odd way so that he almost appeared to be flailing his arms as he ran. And then, maybe twenty or twenty-five feet from where he'd started, the man seized up and fell face-first into the dirt. And there he did not move.

One of the shooters on the hillside had found his target and delivered a fatal shot.

"The numbers are in our favor," Lucy said.

"Yes, but the daylight is not."

- 22 -

The last remnants of daylight exhausted down in the little canyon where the prospectors had built their camp some years ago.

Up on the high ridge there was likely another hour of dusk before full night set on, but down in the canyon the shadows were winning, at least until dawn. At best, Hughes figured he'd be able to see the men behind the trees for maybe another fifteen minutes.

The man out on the path at the entrance to the camp had not moved since he'd fallen. The two injured men behind the pine tree were quiet now. The man who Hughes had shot though the leg had tied something around his thigh and was now doing whatever he could to help the man shot in the shoulder.

Apache Tom and one of the soldiers were still behind pine trees, armed and waiting for their chance. Somewhere in the brush down by the river – unless he had moved – there was still a cavalryman lurking. And up near the entrance to the camp, one of the two lookouts was still in the fight.

"Come dark, they can grab that money and slip out of the camp," Lucy said.

"I suspect that's what they're waiting for," Hughes said.

"It would be a shame, after all this, if they were to get the money and escape."

Hughes let out a heavy breath. Both of them had been fostering the same thoughts as the minutes ticked away and the darkness continued to descend around them. It would be different if Hughes and Lucy were on the outside and the thieves were trapped in the cabin. But it was hard to keep a suspect pinned down when the suspect was outside and free to roam. The only thing keeping Apache Tom and the soldiers at the campsite was that money. They wouldn't leave without it. And they knew, to get it, they just had to wait for nightfall.

"What's he doing?" Lucy asked.

Hughes craned his neck to see. Down in the pine trees, Apache Tom had abandoned his hiding place and was making his way – tree to tree – toward the back of the campsite.

"Going for the horses," Hughes said. "They're planning their escape out there."

Hughes moved around in the shadows of the cabin to try to get a look down at the back of the campsite where Apache Tom and the cavalrymen had tied their horses, but he could not get a vantage through the open door.

"Will they leave without the money?" Lucy asked.

Hughes shook his head.

"I would not think so," he said. "They're wanted men now, and they know it. They've killed for that money, and they've given up any chance of a free life to get that money. Even if they escape now, they'll always be looking over their shoulder. We may be pinned down, but I guarantee you it's the men out there who are feeling trapped. The only thing that gets them out of the trap is that money sitting in those bags right there."

Lucy nodded.

"I agree. The only hope they have of getting far enough away from all this is to have money enough to buy their way to safety. And in a half hour or less, they'll be able to walk right out there and pick it up and walk away."

"Yep."

"We should try for the money," Lucy said.

Hughes looked at her.

"That's a helluva dangerous proposition," he said.

Lucy nodded her head, and in the dim light inside the cabin, Hughes saw a smile break across her face.

"Is it true, Mr. Hughes, that back in California they called you Parlous Cal?"

Hughes shrugged. He'd earned the nickname in standoffs not completely unlike this one. Though most often, he was the one outside with his adversaries trapped inside. Rash exploits that included two-handed gun fights at five or six feet, storming a barricaded position during a shootout – things a younger man did without much thought to personal safety.

"I suppose some folks called me that," Hughes said.

"Well, this might be a situation that calls for perilous activity, Mr. Hughes. Or should I say, Parlous Cal?"

Hughes held his breath for a moment.

"You want me to run out there and grab that money?" Hughes said.

"It's the one thing that guarantees they don't get away."

Hughes leaned forward to where he could see the money outside the door. Fifteen yards, maybe. Maybe a little less. With Apache Tom down collecting the horses, there was only one shooter behind the pine trees. Maybe two, if the cavalryman from the creek bank had come up to join in the fight.

"I could make fifteen yards to grab the money before they can shoot me," Hughes said. "I don't know if I can make fifteen yards back."

"I could try," Lucy suggested.

"No," Hughes said. She might be a Pinkerton detective, but she was still a woman. There was no way that Hughes would allow her to make a dash for that money while he was able to do it.

"You could do a better job of covering me with that

Winchester than I could do of covering you," Lucy said.

"I won't allow it," Hughes said. "You'll have to drag the table clear so I can get a good start out the door."

"I can do that," Lucy said.

"Then let's move before Apache Tom comes back up. The odds are in our favor now."

Lucy set the Schofield on the ground, and Hughes leaned his Winchester against the wall of the cabin. Lucy took hold of one of the table legs and nodded to Hughes.

"Ready?" she asked.

"Go," Hughes said.

With an almighty jerk, Lucy dragged the table clear of the doorway in one big motion. Two big strides, and Parlous Cal was leaping from the rough-hewn porch of the log cabin into the dirt beyond.

Any surprise move will catch an adversary off guard. A man committed to an unexpected course of action has two, maybe three seconds to do what he intends to do before his adversary recovers from the surprise. That was the general rule of thumb that Hughes judged his "parlous" actions by.

He was off the porch in about one second. He'd started his run at a crouch. In the fifth second, he reached out and snatched both money bags, scooping up first one and then the other in one hand.

But stopping to grab the money bags ended the momentum that had dragged Hughes forward, and now he had to shift to go back the other way. That was another second, and in the sixth second a shot snapped from behind a pine tree. Hughes felt the bullet as it tore through the tail of his canvas duster, tugging at the coat.

He started back toward the cabin and the rifle behind him barked a second time. He was keeping himself low, in a crouch, hoping to make himself a smaller target, but he was throwing too much weight forward as he tried to run and then his feet were caught in a tangle with each other. It felt like someone kicked his heel as he tried to run, and Hughes stumbled and began to topple over.

He landed on his elbows, instinctively throwing his forearms out to catch himself, and the money bags were under him now. A third shot missed, sailing over him where he was sprawled on the ground. Hughes pushed himself up and made a stumbling run toward the porch. He fell again, skidding onto the rough porch of the cabin. He didn't try to get back up. Hughes threw the money bags ahead of him into the cabin and then half-crawled, half-clambered through the door of the cabin.

"Are you hit?" Lucy asked.

"Shove that table back," Hughes said, rolling away from the open doorway.

The fact was, he did not know if he was shot or not. He heard the table slide as Lucy strained against it to push it back into place, and then she was beside him, on her knees, feeling his legs.

"It looked like he shot your leg out from under you," Lucy said.

"Yeah, I thought I felt something jerk against my leg, and then I tripped over my own feet."

He felt Lucy's hands wrapped around his leg, up and down one leg, then up and down the other. She repeated it, sliding her hands from thigh to foot. Her hands moved over his boot and then stopped.

"He shot you in the heel of your boot," Lucy said.

Hughes sat up and looked down at his foot. Indeed, the heel of his boot had been shot away. No wonder he'd stumbled and gone down.

"Now what?" Lucy asked.

"Well, now when they want to get the money before they make a run, they'll have to come into the cabin. So we should prepare for that."

Hughes looked through the debris inside the cabin and found a tin bucket. He broke up some pieces of wooden furniture and used his knife to shave thin pieces from a chair. Lucy, pressed against the inside wall of the cabin, kept a watch outside the door.

"I'm going to start a fire in this bucket and push it into the corner there," Hughes said. "If someone tries to come through that door, we'll see them coming. We can stay back in the shadows."

Hughes had broken up a couple of chairs. He had a good pile of wood shavings and had found a piece of burlap that he wadded up to use to get the fire going.

He struck a match and lit the burlap in the bottom of the tin bucket, pushing the wood shavings up to it. He had a little flame going in a moment, and then he started adding slightly larger pieces of wood that he'd cut away from pieces of furniture. But then Lucy made a noise at the doorway.

"I think you can forgo that," she said.

Hughes looked up at her and saw Lucy raising up the Schofield, cocking back the hammer. Hughes snatched his Winchester from the floor beside him.

"There is movement in the trees," Lucy said.

Hughes squatted low and peered over the table through the open door.

In a gap in the trees, Hughes could see horses moving down close to the creek. Nearer, though, in the area where Apache Tom had been hiding behind a pine tree, there were figures moving among the shadows. He thought he could see three or four men.

"Is that all of them?" Hughes asked.

"I think the one from the brush down by the creek has joined them. Maybe the one who was up by the path. It looks like they're getting ready to make a charge."

Hughes took a breath.

"We can back up to the back of the cabin, pick them off as they come through the door. Or we can try to get them as they make their run."

"Let's take them from here," Lucy said.

And then, immediately.

"Oh! Now!"

The men had broken clear of the pines and were running hard for the cabin.

Lucy fired the Schofield once and Apache Tom spun, clearly hit, but he kept coming. Hughes did not even have the Winchester in his shoulder yet. But then all hell erupted from somewhere outside the cabin.

Albert Fears, Dan Tucker, and Corporal Greaves had moved down closer to the campsite. They'd taken up positions, and when Apache Tom and the three cavalrymen made their charge, the two lawmen and the corporal opened up.

In the space of three heartbeats it was all over. The cavalrymen tossed down their weapons and dropped to their knees, their hands and forearms covering their heads.

Apache Tom, who had been on the flank nearest to Albert Fears and the others, had taken the worst of the shooting. He was shot twice in the chest, once in the neck, and Lucy's shot with the Schofield had caught him in the gut. The other three men were uninjured, but when Apache Tom finally spun and dropped to the ground, it was enough to make the men surrender.

- 23 -

"We never did see no sign of Lieutenant Stellman," Corporal Greaves said as he held Calvin Hughes tied a body onto one of the spare horses.

They were working at night now, but Albert Fears had rounded up several discarded tin buckets and lit fires in them so that there was light to see by.

Three men were dead. Apache Tom was likely dead before he hit the ground. The man Hughes shot in the shoulder bled out. And the man who'd been a lookout was shot several times, and he died where he fell.

So they tied the bodies to three of the spare horses.

The cavalryman who Hughes had shot in the leg was going to have an uncomfortable ride back to Silver City, but he'd stuffed a bandanna through both the entry and exit wounds, and so long as it did not infect, he would survive his injury.

The other three men sat near a bucket with a fire burning inside it. Dangerous Dan Tucker kept a watch on them, though their wrists were all in handcuffs behind their backs.

"We'll catch up with him sooner or later," Hughes vowed. "And one or all of those men are going to testify that he was the brains behind this job."

Greaves nodded.

"What will happen to them?" he asked.

"Prison. Probably for a long time."

"And Stellman?"

"If they testify against him, put him as the leader, he'll hang," Hughes said.

"If you catch him."

"We'll catch him," Hughes said. "He killed two Wells Fargo men."

While Hughes and Greaves dealt with the bodies, Lucy Blake pushed one of the tin buckets toward the hole where the man had dug up the money. She used the shovel and scooted away pine straw until she found a second hole. The started to turn dirt until she came up with other debris – wigs and clothes. Albert Fears helped her, and soon they'd uncovered four vests similar in fashion to those typically worn by Apache men, six animal-skin britches, and six wigs. These were the disguises used to fool Kays and Billy, the men on the stagecoach who witnessed the "Indians" making their escape from the burning relay station.

"We've got the money and the disguises," Lucy Blake said to the four prisoners. "Which one of you is going to testify against the others?"

The men all sat mute. In front of each other, they wouldn't turn on each other. But a few days in separate jail cells, facing the possibility of a hanging, they might have a change of heart.

Albert Fears fashioned three torches, using what he could find around the camp, and within the hour the bizarre group was on the trail leading out to the road.

Corporal Greaves led the group, a torch in hand and trailing the leads of the spare horses and the three with the bodies tied to them.

The prisoners followed the spare horses, with Dan Tucker and Calvin Hughes riding behind them. Tucker and Hughes both had six-shooters in their hands, watching for any of the prisoners to try to go on escape. Hughes had the Santa Rita payroll bags riding behind his saddle on Sequoia.

Lucy Blake followed behind with a torch held high to help Tucker and Hughes watch the prisoners. Lucy had wrapped the disguises in a blanket and tied the bundle of evidence to a spare horse.

And Albert Fears, riding his big draught horse, rode behind, also holding a torch.

They walked the entire way back to Silver City. The horses were all spent, none of them much willing to do a late-night ride through the darkness. And it was safer to walk – to avoid any of the horses stepping into a hole, to avoid any of the prisoners trying to flee.

They rode through most of the night, entering a quiet and dark Silver City just before dawn, and there Hughes and Dan Tucker installed the four prisoners in Tucker's jail and sent for a doctor to take a look at the wounded man.

***

After a couple of hours of sleep at the Palace Hotel, Calvin Hughes dressed and went to the Wells Fargo office to speak to Casper Bennett. He took the Santa Rita payroll with him, and walked past the stagecoach as the driver and shotgun rider worked to strap luggage onto the top. There was a small crowd gathered to see the coach off. Hughes scanned the faces of those nearby, but did not see Lieutenant Stellman.

It was a long shot, he realized. The lieutenant would have been foolish to try to get on the stagecoach when, by now, every lawman in three counties was looking for him. He'd be better off hiding up in the mountains for a few weeks and then trying to sneak out of town when nobody was particularly thinking about him.

Still, as he walked by the coach, Hughes poked his head in the window to be sure Stellman was not already aboard.

"We arrested most of that outfit who killed your uncle," Hughes said. He set the money bags down on the counter in the office.

"Who was it?" Bennett asked.

"Soldiers from Fort Bayard," Hughes said. "It looks like a lieutenant over there figured out that the Santa Rita payroll was doubled up and in the safe at the relay station, and he concocted the plan."

"So it never was Apache raiders?" Casper Bennett asked.

"Never was," Hughes said. "They took the safe up to an abandoned mining camp and busted it open there. They buried the money and their disguises at the camp. We caught them there late yesterday, but the lieutenant who appears to be the ringleader got away."

"Got away?" Casper said.

"We think he was planning to meet the others, but it turned into a shooting match, and my best guess is that he heard the shots and fled."

"Where is he now?"

Hughes pushed the bags toward Casper Bennett.

"Count the money and put those in the safe for the Santa Rita mine," Hughes said. "I'll need a receipt so that when it comes time for the trial, I can prove I gave you the money."

"Sure," Casper said. "But what about the other one? The ringleader that got away?"

"His name is Stellman. He mustered out of the cavalry yesterday. Wells Fargo will catch him. Eventually. He'll turn up somewhere, and I promise you a Wells Fargo man will be there."

"I hope you're right," Casper Bennett said, clearly disappointed that one of the men responsible for his uncle's murder was still loose.

"I'll say this to you, Casper. I hope when Lieutenant Stellman is caught, I'm the Wells Fargo man who is there to do it. I've been all through your uncle's ledgers, and I'll say to you that he was a good man, an honest man, and he didn't deserve what happened to him. I'd like to be able to say that I'm the man that brought his killer to justice."

Once the stagecoach had left and the Santa Rita payroll was inside the Wells Fargo safe in Silver City, Calvin Hughes walked down to the jail.

Dan Tucker was standing at the stove, pouring himself a cup of coffee that looked thick enough to float a horseshoe.

"Do you ever sleep?" Hughes said.

Tucker grinned at him.

"Eleven o'clock in the morning to three o'clock in the afternoon," Tucker said. "Those are my sleeping hours. It's about the only time during the day or night that there ain't some outlaw wandering about who needs shooting. The rest of the time, I try to be ready."

"So an hour to bedtime?" Hughes asked.

"About that," Tucker said. "Private Johnson has been asking for you."

"Who is Private Johnson?" Hughes said.

"He's the man you drilled through the leg yesterday. He's in the back room, on a cot, where the doctor was looking at him. When I got ready to take him back to the cells, he said he wanted to talk to the Wells Fargo man."

"Well, let's go talk to him," Hughes said.

In a back office, the soldier with the wound to his

leg was laying on his back on a canvas cot, a blanket covering him and his arms wrapped under the cot and his wrists handcuffed together.

"Private Johnson?" Hughes said.

The man's eyes were half closed, but they snapped open now.

"Wells Fargo," he said. "Just the man I wanted to see."

"How can I help you?"

The private started to chuckle.

"I sure am glad you're not a better shot than what you are. We might not be having this conversation."

Hughes grinned and nodded.

"Maybe. But if you'd stuck your head instead of your ass in the air, I'd have put that round between your eyes."

Johnson chuckled again.

"What can you give me?" Johnson asked.

"For testimony? Five years in a territorial prison."

Johnson swallowed hard.

"I'd rather do two."

"Two men were killed," Hughes said. "If you wanted to do two years in prison, you'd have tied them up instead of killing them."

Johnson nodded his head without lifting it from the cot.

"All right. Five years. Stellman planned it all out.

That man from the mine, Cushman, he was in the saloon at Fort Bayard complaining about the payroll. Stellman heard him. Asked about it. Found out that they would end up with two months of payroll at the relay station safe, and he started figuring it was going to coincide with the time when we mustered out and when he mustered out. He talked us into helping him. Said there was no way we'd get caught if we dressed like Apache. Said he and Apache Tom could lead the posse down to the Rio Grande and then arrange to lose the tracks and that would be that."

"You burned the relay station thinking no one would miss the safe, at least not for a while."

"That's right," Johnson said. "It was all Stellman's idea. Killing them two men. Dressing up like Apache. Riding off when we saw the stagecoach. He even picked the place for us to break into the safe."

"Why didn't you just camp there?" Hughes said. "Why come to Silver City?"

"We figured it was best not to be where the money was. If we made camp up there at those cabins, it might bring someone looking to see who was around."

"Where is Stellman going?" Hughes asked.

"Denver. He's got a girl waiting for him in Denver. Used to talk about her all the time."

"What about Missouri?"

Johnson shook his head.

"I don't know nothing about Missouri," he said.

"Stellman told me his folks have a place in Missouri."

Johnson started to chuckle again.

"No. That's a lie. He's from Ohio. Not no Missouri. I'm telling you, he'll make for Denver."

"All right, Private Johnson," Hughes said. "I'll talk to the prosecutor and work it out for you. If you testify, he'll ask the judge to give you five years."

"What about them others, the ones in the jail cell?"

Hughes shrugged.

"I don't reckon any of them will do less than fifteen years."

Johnson pursed his lips together and closed his eyes. It was hard to tell if he regretted the misfortune of his friends, or if the knowledge of their likely sentences satisfied him that he'd made the right decision to talk.

- 24 -

The man stepped from the stagecoach and took a furtive look around at the people nearby.

He'd come through this way about two years prior, before the railroad tracks were finished to Albuquerque. At the time, he'd taken the railroad as far as Las Vegas. There he boarded a stagecoach bound for Silver City. The coach would take him to his posting at Fort Bayard. The coach stopped in Albuquerque, though. He remembered it differently. He remembered a plaza and several old buildings. A mission.

This place was a new town, built opposite the railroad tracks, and it was all unfamiliar to him.

A quick look around at the people nearby gave him a sense of peace. He did not see a face he recognized.

Those who were nearby, either waiting to greet passengers on the coach or waiting for an expected letter or parcel, they noted the man who got off the stagecoach. He was a young man, red cheeks and a patchy beard that suggested he was still too young to grow a proper beard but even so it had been several weeks since he'd touched his face with a razor. They noted, too, the wild look about him. His clothes were not clean. He was thin, as if he'd fought for every recent meal and lost too many of the fights. His eyes darted nervously, and when a couple of men down the road gave up a cheer for some private joke, the man from the stagecoach started like a spooked coyote.

"Can I help you, partner?"

The man jumped again and turned to find the stagecoach driver standing a couple of feet away from him.

"No."

"You look lost, son," the stagecoach driver said. "Do you need something? Can I help you in some way?"

"I just need to get to the train depot."

The jehu's face broke into a broad smile, clearly amused at the young man's nervousness and befuddled by whatever plight he found himself in.

"Well, the depot is hard to miss," he said. "It's just across the thoroughfare, right there."

The young man with the dirty clothes looked around at the depot.

"Yes. I see it. Thank you."

He dropped his head and started across the street towards the depot. The jehu watched him go.

"I guess you see all kinds," the jehu said. "But that one there is one of the stranger ones."

His shotgun rider, who had missed the conversation between the driver and the passenger, glanced up to see who he was referring to. He saw the man with his head pointed toward the ground walking across the thoroughfare toward the train depot.

"Well, he didn't cause no trouble. Probably just a prospector who didn't have no luck. Tucked his tail and heading home."

The jehu nodded agreement, and the two men went on about their business. They had baggage to unload from the coach, and more baggage to put on. The clock always ran against the whip and shotgun as they tried to keep to the Wells Fargo schedule.

The rough looking man who disembarked from the stagecoach gave a false name to his fellow passengers, and then through quiet demeanor signaled to them that he did not care to give them any other information. Like the stagecoach men, the other passengers just thought he was odd.

In truth, the man had spent a month living in the hills north of Silver City. He used some of his payout from the army to buy his clothes off a prospector down in a camp. All he had to wear otherwise was the uniform that marked him not just as a cavalryman, but also as a wanted man. In a little village north of Silver City, he bought supplies enough to see him through for the month. When his beard had filled in a little – as much as his youth would allow – and he thought maybe people around Silver City wouldn't be looking out for him, he made his way into town and purchased a ticket for the stagecoach to Albuquerque.

He had enough money for the stage to Albuquerque, and enough for the train to Denver. When he reached Denver it would be rough going, but he figured he could change his name and find work. What he did not know is if his girl there would still have him. Did she even know he was wanted?

So now he crossed the thoroughfare from the Wells Fargo office to the train depot to buy his ticket for Denver, for his new life. It wasn't going to be what he hoped. His take from that Santa Rita payroll would have set him up real well, but now he had next to nothing. But if he could make his way to Denver, Stellman believed at least he would not hang, and that was the alternative if he got caught.

Already the train at the station was hissing steam, and thick black smoke rose from the smokestack at the front of the engine. In twenty minutes that train would be rolling toward Denver, and Stellman would be rolling toward freedom.

He was halfway across the thoroughfare when he saw, too late, from the corner of his eye a man approaching him quickly.

Stellman picked up his head and turned to look at the man.

He had so convinced himself that he was on his way to freedom, even as Lieutenant Stellman realized that he recognized Calvin Hughes walking toward him, he still failed to fully appreciate his predicament.

"Lieutenant Stellman," Hughes called out, still approaching the man from about fifteen feet away. The Wells Fargo man was wearing a dark suit and a dark hat. Over the suit he wore a canvas duster. The duster was pushed back on one side, exposing Hughes' Schofield. His hand rested easily on the grip of the six-shooter. The leather thong that went over the hammer was flapping loose. Hughes would ready to clear leather.

"You've got me confused," Stellman said, and he started to turn back toward the depot.

"Like hell, Stellman," Hughes said. "I know you, and I'm here to arrest you."

As he glanced toward the depot, Stellman saw a woman standing there. She was dressed smart in a split riding skirt, a dark blouse and a dark coat. She wore a black eye patch over one eye, and she was toting in her gloved hand a small, 2-shot pocket pistol.

Beside her was a giant of a man, well over six feet and toting a heavy build. The man wore a mustache and a bowler hat that looked almost ridiculous on his large frame. He held a scattergun with two short barrels.

Stellman also recognized the two Pinkerton detectives.

The former cavalry officer's mind raced as he tried to think of a way out. He stood his ground, facing the Pinkertons, but his head tilted toward the Wells Fargo agent who was nearly to him now.

"I'm going to have to ask you for that sidearm, Lieutenant."

Stellman did not move.

"How'd you find me?" he said.

"The Wells Fargo agent in Silver City, the man you bought the ticket from. He sent me a telegram yesterday. Said a suspicious man came in and bought a ticket to Albuquerque."

"And you got here first?" Stellman said.

Hughes nodded his head back toward the Wells Fargo office.

"I work here in Albuquerque, Mr. Stellman. I was already here. When you decided to run, you picked the wrong place to run to."

For the space of several heartbeats, the foursome remained frozen in place. Hughes, his hand resting casually on the Schofield. Albert Fears, the shotgun in both hands crossing his body, ready to drop and shoot in a moment's notice. Lucy Blake, the two-shot gun half hidden in the folds of her skirt.

And Stellman, indecisive, a gun on his hip and a noose around his neck. If he did not feel the fibers of the rope, it was simply a matter of time.

"That gun, Mr. Stellman. I'm going to need you to slide it from the holster, easily, and hand it over."

Hughes held out his left hand, almost close enough to touch now. His right hand rested easily on the grip of the Schofield.

Stellman bit his lip and sighed heavily. He raised up his left hand to his face, rubbing it roughly over his forehead and eyes.

"Don't do it," Hughes said. He recognized the indecision, he could see as if reading a book the options that passed through Stellman's mind. They were fast narrowing. "Give up and take your chances with the judge."

Stellman's hand dropped to the sidearm, a Colt Army. He flung himself backwards, away from Hughes. Away from Albert Fears and Lucy Blake. He jerked the Colt loose from its holster and started to swing it toward Hughes.

But the Wells Fargo man had already pulled the Schofield clear of the holster. In a clean, swift motion he cocked the hammer as he brought the gun to bear. Even shooting from the hip he wasn't going to miss. Stellman was too near.

The Schofield belched smoke as the hammer fell. The boom of the gun echoed along the thoroughfare. The shot struck Stellman in the ribs. Hughes squeezed the trigger a second time, raising the gun higher as he did. The second shot hit Stellman in the chest. And again, the third shot following the second along an almost identical path.

The three punches from the Schofield rattled the man, staggered him, and he stumbled back another several steps before falling to the ground.

His Colt Army hit the ground beside him, and Hughes moved quickly and kicked the gun away. Then he dropped down and took Stellman by the hand.

"Hang on Lieutenant," Hughes said.

But Stellman was already spluttering blood. He'd chosen a bullet instead of a rope. Hughes couldn't blame him.

- 25 -

"I saw the money first," Lucy Blake said.

"I risked my life running out there under fire to grab the bags and bring them back into the cabin," Hughes said.

Albert Blake chuckled.

The three of them stood at the bar in R. H. Greenleaf's restaurant.

"It's a picnic, down by the river, and we don't do it until spring," Lucy Blake said, presenting her case in a matter-of-fact fashion as if it was indisputable. "I arrived first at the campsite. I witnessed the man dig the money out of the ground. I was the first among us to lay eyes on the Santa Rita payroll. I win the bet."

Hughes took a sip of his beer, and then he shook his head, setting the beer heavily on the bar.

"I recall clearly that the bet was whichever of us recovered the money," Hughes said. "Mr. Fears, can you not help provide some clarification here?"

Albert Fears grinned and shook his head.

"I'm not an objective party," he said. "I was looking forward to the springtime picnic down by the river."

Hughes scoffed.

"You are just looking forward to a free meal."

Fears shrugged his shoulders.

"Could be that I am. But either way, I'm not impartial."

"But as a reasonable man, you can obviously agree that when I ran out of that cabin and grabbed the sacks of money, that — by the very definition of the word — was recovering the money," Hughes said. "Whereas, Miss Blake witnessing the thieves digging up the money is simply seeing the money, and not recovering it."

Albert Fears shrugged his shoulders.

"It would be unseemly for me to rule against my own partner," Albert Fears said.

Hughes took another drink from his beer, draining the mug. He set the mug down on the bar and turned away from his two companions.

"I believe the terms of the wager were altered,"

Calvin Hughes said. "Or possibly never given in good faith from the start."

Lucy Blake groaned.

"I resent that implication," she said. "No one is attempting to cheat you, Mr. Hughes. We simply want our picnic."

"Then we'll call it a draw," Hughes said. "You can buy me my dinner tonight, without Mr. Fears' company. And come spring, I'll owe you both a picnic."

"By the river," Fears grinned.

"Yes. By the river."

Lucy Blake smiled at patted Hughes on the arm.

"I'll accept a draw," she said.

the end

ABOUT THE AUTHOR

Robert Peecher is the author of more than two score of Western novels. He is former journalist who spent 20 years working as a reporter and editor for daily and weekly newspapers in Georgia.

Together with his wife Jean, he's raised three fine boys and a mess of dogs. An avid outdoorsman who enjoys hiking trails and paddling rivers, Peecher's novels are inspired by a combination of his outdoor adventures, his fascination with American history, and his love of the one truly American genre of novel: The Western.

For more information and to keep up with his latest releases, we would encourage you to visit his website (mooncalfpress.com) and sign up for his twice-monthly e-newsletter.

OTHER NOVELS BY ROBERT PEECHER

THE LODERO WESTERNS: Two six-shooters and a black stallion. When Lodero makes a graveside vow to track down the mystery of his father's disappearance, it sends Lodero and Juan Carlos Baca on an epic quest through the American Southwest. Don't miss this great 4-book series!

THE TWO RIVERS STATION WESTERNS: Jack Bell refused to take the oath from the Yankees at Bennett Place. Instead, he stole a Union cavalry horse and started west toward a new life in Texas. There he built a town and raised a family, but he'll have to protect his way of life behind a Henry rifle and a Yankee Badge.

ANIMAS FORKS: Animas Forks, Colorado, is the largest city in west of the Mississippi (at 14,000 feet). The town has everything you could want in a Frontier Boomtown: cutthroats, ne'er-do-wells, whores, backshooters, drunks, thieves, and murderers. Come on home to Animas Forks in this fun, character-driven series.

TRULOCK'S POSSE: When the Garver gang guns down the town marshal, Deputy Jase Trulock must form a posse to chase down the Garvers before they reach the outlaw town of Profanity.

FIND THESE AND OTHER NOVELS BY
ROBERT PEECHER AT AMAZON.COM

Made in the USA
Las Vegas, NV
15 December 2021